COME HOME TO THE RANCH

RETURN TO BLESSING, TEXAS
BOOK TWO

LACEY DAVIS

Return to Blessing, Texas

Come Home to the Cowboys
Come Home to the Ranch
Come Home to the Lawmen
Come Home to the Country
Come Home to the Doctor's
Come Home to the Bride
Return to Blessing, Texas Books 1-3
Return to Blessing, Texas Books 4-6

Want to learn about my new releases before anyone else? Sign up for my New Book Alert and receive a complimentary book. Blindfold Me.

The Maid of Honor Snags the Groomsmen

Lonely, Stacey wants the happiness and family her friend has, but is she willing to take the risk and embrace a different way of life?

Recently returned to Blessing, Texas, Navy SEAL Luis Nash came home with a secret that could destroy his sanity. Only his best friend and fellow groomsman Trevor Garcia knows and he's made them billions.

When Luis sees Stacey, he knows she's exactly what he needs. And when he rescues her from a prank, she agrees to his demands.

Only problem...spending an entire week together in bliss had only made Luis want more. And Luis's secret could destroy everything, sending Stacey fleeing back to New York.

CHAPTER 1

Stacy Rivera stared at her friend. She'd never seen her happier. The lucky bitch had just married her men and she understood why she was happy. The ranch was wonderful. Her husbands were so damn handsome, it was unbelievable.

It had taken her a while, but now Kalie had everything she'd ever wanted except for a family, and from the way they acted like rabbits, that should be happening soon.

A man walked up beside her.

"Ma'am, I need you to come with me," he said.

Turning, she gazed at him, her brows raising. "Whatever for?"

"You're under arrest," he said.

She started laughing. "Did Kalie put you up to this?"

"No, ma'am," he said. "I work with the Texas Rangers and I've been watching you undercover."

"Well good for you," she said laughing. "I haven't done anything wrong. I'm not going with you. Besides, this is my friend's wedding. I'm waiting to catch the bouquet and then I'll be getting into my rental car and going back to San Antonio for the night. Tomorrow, I fly back to New York."

The man sighed. "Are you coming with me or not?"

"No," she said.

The man had on a suit coat and a dark hat, and his emerald eyes were dark.

Just then a second man walked up. "Is she the one?"

"She's our perp," the man said.

"Are you guys serious?" she said.

They surrounded her and then she felt the slip of the handcuffs on her wrist.

"Hey," she said.

"Let's go," the man in the dark hat said.

"I want to see a badge."

Suddenly a man stepped out of the shadows in front of them.

"What are you doing?"

The two men grinned. "Having fun."

"Let her go," he said. She gazed at him. He had the most gorgeous head of hair with streaks of gray in it. His eyes were an intense shade of jade.

She felt the handcuffs release and the two young men grinned.

"We meant no harm. It's just a prank we like to play," one of them said.

"Get out of here," the man told them.

After they were gone, she glanced at him.

"Sorry about that. They're my younger brothers. They get into mischief."

Stacy gazed at the man. "And who are you?"

"I'm Luis Nash, Preston's older brother," he said. "I just came home from the Navy. I own the Rocking B Ranch."

Just then another man walked up beside him. "Who is this?"

"Stacy Rivera," she said. "I'm Kalie's friend."

"Trevor Garcia," the man said, his dark eyes skimming over her, sending a ripple of desire through her.

Those dark brown eyes were filled with a sexual heat.

"You were the maid of honor," Luis said as he moved a little closer.

"Yes," she replied. Glancing at the two of them, her heart beating a little faster. There was something so damn attractive about these two handsome cowboys.

She'd been here a week and during that time, she'd learned so much about this little community. And she was curious about what happened between a woman and two men.

"I guess our little town is quite shocking to a woman from New York City," Luis said.

Shaking her head, she sighed. "No, it's made me curious. I want to learn more about how this life is. I'd like to experience two men at once. I'd like to learn more about living this way."

Why was she telling them this? She couldn't believe those words had just come from between her lips.

The two men glanced at each other.

"Where are you spending the night?" Luis asked.

"At a hotel in San Antonio," she replied, thinking of the two-hour drive ahead of her.

"Do you really want to experience two men at the same time?" Trevor asked.

"Yes," she said, knowing that this was her opportunity to

experience what she'd only imagined. "I'd like to spend a week being shown what this life is like. For someone to teach me the ropes."

The two men surrounded her.

"We'd like to show you," Trevor said.

"Can you stay another week?" Luis asked.

Her heart leaped into her throat. The smell of each man drifted to her and she closed her eyes, inhaling their scent. She might be fired from her job, but she didn't care.

"Yes," she gasped.

"And you want to learn," Luis said. "Because once you come home with us, you're ours for the week."

Her breath shuddered in her throat. Was she really going to do this?

"Yes," she gasped.

"Take your panties off," Trevor said.

"Right here? Now?"

"Yes, now," Luis demanded.

Swallowing, she wondered what she'd just agreed to.

"No commitments?" she asked, reaching up under her skirt and pulling her underwear down.

"None," they both replied.

"Will you both be sleeping with me?"

"Yes," they both answered.

"Time to leave," Luis said, taking her by the arm. "Time to take you home and fuck you."

Oh, dear, there would be no preliminaries. No warm-up or *let's get to know you.*

"Let me tell Kalie good-bye and then I'll follow you to your ranch," she said.

"I'll drive your car," Trevor said. "You ride with Luis."

What the hell was she doing? She'd never been so bold, but then again, maybe this was what she'd been waiting for.

Kalie had found her happily ever after here in Blessing. Maybe she would too.

CHAPTER 2

*L*uis helped Stacy into his truck. Her friend had grinned when she saw them leaving together and he knew that if Preston wasn't leaving for his honeymoon, Luis would've been hearing from him.

And that was fine. But it was his brother's wedding night, and tomorrow they left on their honeymoon, he felt certain Preston was busy.

Gazing at the woman sitting nervously waiting for him to shut the door, heat filled him, going straight to his crotch. He'd been watching her all night and wondered how he could convince her to come home with him. It'd been way easier than he expected.

Even Trevor seemed pleased at how she was curious about their lifestyle.

Shutting the door, he walked to his side of the truck and quickly climbed in. One glance at her and he could tell she was having second thoughts. Somehow he had to make her feel at ease with her decision. Because he couldn't wait to get her home and show her just how attracted he'd been to her all night long.

"You don't know me, but my parents raised me to treat a woman right. There would be hell to pay from my brothers and my father if Trevor and I mistreated you. So sit back and relax."

She licked her lips. "Thank you. It's just I often get myself into trouble by making a rash decision. This one was instantaneous and one of my quickest agreements. But after watching Kalie this week, I had to know."

He grinned at her. "If it makes you feel any better, all night I've watched you and wondered how I could get you alone. Mission accomplished."

Reaching over, he took her arm and tugged her to the middle of the seat, next to him, sweet womanly scent reaching his nose. Up against his thigh, her body snuggled into his. He wanted to touch her. It had been so long since he'd taken a woman, and tonight he could hardly wait.

The road to his place was rough and often there were deer in the ditch. Tonight, he just hoped that none of them would decide to jump the fence and run in front of his truck. Because he knew he was distracted.

Very distracted by the beautiful blonde sitting next to him.

Laying his hand on her knee, he pushed her skirt up and she gasped. His fingers trailed up her leg, feeling her soft silky skin. When his fingers reached her center, she was bare and he couldn't help but smile.

His finger trailed over her clit and she jumped.

It was hard to tease her and also watch the road. He really wanted to pull over, put the truck in park, and take her right here and now. Spread her out on the seat and act like he was eighteen, not thirty-five.

"Pull your dress over your head," he told her, wanting to see her breasts.

Glancing at him, her brows drew together in a frown and she hesitated.

"Darling, don't stop and think. That will earn you a spanking. When we give you a command, you are to immediately do what we ask. I'll give you a pass this time, but next time, I'll turn your ass pink."

"But you're driving," she said.

"And I want you naked," he replied. "No one is out here on these country roads this time of night. So strip."

"But..."

"Don't argue with me, do it," he said in a stern voice. "This is what you agreed to. This is what the next week will be like."

Reluctantly she unzipped the back of her dress and then pulled it over her head. Since they had already removed her panties, all that remained were her heels and her bra. Reaching behind her she unclipped her bra and let it slide slowly off exposing her luscious breasts.

In the moonlight, shadows danced over her naked skin.

"You can leave the heels on," he said.

As much as she said she wanted this, through the dim lighting from the dashboard, he could see the doubts forming in those beautiful blue eyes of hers.

He pulled her face toward his and gave her a quick peck on the lips. It was short and sweet, and not near like how he wanted to kiss her. There would be time for a deeper all-consuming mating of their lips once they reached their ranch. But for now, this would have to do.

"Beautiful," he said. "Take your fingers and play with your clit."

She licked her lips and swallowed but did as he said.

"Spread your legs, I want to see you come," he said. "Before we reach the ranch. You have less than five minutes. If you don't come for me, you'll be punished."

Closing her eyes, he kept glancing down as she fingered herself with one hand. He reached over and twisted her nipples with his fingers. Her breathing was changing, she was gasping for air.

"When you come, say my name," he said, longing to hear her moans.

A groan escaped her, the sound reverberating inside his truck. The smell of sweet pussy filled the air and he couldn't wait to get to the ranch.

"Luis," she gasped, her body tensing.

"That's it, baby, open your eyes and look at me," he coaxed. The next time she orgasmed, he wanted her screaming his name, her voice filled with passion.

Her legs were spread wide and she grunted, the sound so pleasant in the truck. It had been so long since he'd heard a woman in the throes of passion.

With a cry, her body shuddered, her hips arching up off the seat of his truck. Unable to resist, he reached down and swatted her on the pussy and she shuddered again.

"Good timing," he said as he turned onto the lane with a big arch over it that read the Rocking B Ranch.

The gate slowly swung open and he drove through.

"Give me your hand," he said. "I want to lick your fingers."

Staring at him, she raised her hand to his mouth and he

took her fingers and licked them. "You taste mighty sweet. I can't wait to explore that sweet pussy of yours."

Leaning back against the seat, she sighed, the sound filled with contentment. But not for long. Once he got her in the house, they were going to explore every inch of her feminine curves.

Already at the house, Trevor leaned against her car when they pulled up in front of the house. Throwing the truck in park, he scrambled out of the seat.

"Wait and let me get your door," he said.

When he stepped out of the truck, he nodded toward Trevor. "It's going to be a hell of a night."

The man smiled and hurried into the house. He would prepare the bed, gather their toys, and get ready for their evening. Luis walked around and opened Stacy's door. He took her hand and helped her alight and then he lifted her and slung her over his shoulder.

"What are you doing?"

"I'm carrying you into the house and straight up to the bedroom," he said. "Trevor is getting everything ready."

She swallowed hard and he knew she was nervous. But he would do everything he could to put her at ease.

Hauling her up the stairs, he rubbed his hand over her backside. The woman had nice ample curves. Curves that he couldn't wait to explore. And a beautiful sparkling white ass that he longed to turn pink.

When he reached the bedroom, the door was closed. He set her on her feet in the hallway and gazed at her. The light was on and he let his eyes feast on her naked beauty. She slung her blonde hair back and her sapphire eyes stared at him.

"Darling, when we're in the bedroom, we're in control. You will obey us at all times or you'll be punished. And believe me, Trevor loves to dish out a good spanking, so obey. If you're in pain, your safe word is blue. We will never hurt you intentionally. We want to give you pleasure and receive pleasure from you. We want to make this the best night of your life."

Standing there naked except for those gorgeous silver heels she wore, her eyes sparkled in the light.

"Will you both take me at the same time?"

"Not until you're ready," he said. "But we will share you. If you're not screaming our names when you come, then we haven't done our job. And our desire is to give you the best experience of your life. Tell us what you like and what you don't."

She bit her bottom lip and that little action almost drove him over the edge.

"Do you agree to these terms?"

"Yes," she said. "Just don't hurt me."

"Never," he replied. "Now we have some props in the room that we like to use. They may look scary, but you're going to love them."

Her brows drew together and she nodded.

He took out a handkerchief. "This first night, I'm going to cover your eyes so you experience nothing but pleasure. I want you to focus on the desire you're experiencing, not what you're seeing."

"Oh," she said, sounding disappointed when he placed the blindfold around her eyes. "But I can't see your cock."

He chuckled, pleased she wanted to see the two of them.

"No, but you'll be able to feel them. Now concentrate on the feelings you experience and nothing else."

Luis opened the door and led the blindfolded woman inside where Trevor had laid out all the toys. Tonight was about showing Stacy it was all about her. Her enjoyment. Her desires. And he wanted to hear her screaming his name when she came.

At the wedding, he'd watched her all evening, wondering how he could get her home and in their bed. No matter where he looked, his gaze returned to her like he was drawn to her.

Trevor was already naked.

Luis trailed his lips across her and down her neck to her shoulder where he lightly bit her. Her skin was like satin, smooth and silky.

She moaned.

Handing her off to Trevor, Luis began by tossing his suit coat over a chair and removing his shirt. Next came his belt buckle and he unzipped his pants before he sat in a chair and removed his boots. Once his cowboy boots were off, he shucked his pants and underwear, eager for tonight's festivities.

"Lie down on the bed, darling," Trevor said as he led her to the big bed they had made just for this purpose. It was big enough for three people to share. Big enough for them to have plenty of room for sex.

Reaching out, she sank down on the bed.

"Time for you to suck my cock," Trevor told her.

"What?"

"Put your lips around my cock and suck on the head," he commanded as he pulled her mouth to his cock and she tentatively put her mouth on his rock-hard organ.

With her unable to see, Trevor had to help her.

"Now run your tongue around it and suck on the bulb," he said with a moan.

As she sucked on Trevor's cock, Luis sank down on the big bed and moved behind her. His fingers reached for her clit, teasing the little bud, causing her to tighten around his fingers as they moved over the lips. She moaned and Trevor jerked.

"Oh, darling, that feels so good. Twist her clit again," he said.

Luis thrust his fingers into her pussy and she moaned all over Trevor's cock. Pushing her down on the bed, Trevor followed her, his dick still in her mouth. Luis's hands spread her thighs before placing his mouth against her pussy.

"That's it, suck it," Trevor said. As his head rolled back, Luis knew it wouldn't be long before he would explode.

Luis's hands gripped her hips as his tongue worked its magic on her clit. She groaned and lifted her hips wanting more, and he was happy to comply with her wishes.

Trevor grabbed her head and pushed his cock farther into her mouth as he moved her head up and down, fucking her sweet cheeks. Soon, Trevor would be coming and Luis wondered how Stacy would react to his friend's seed spilling down her throat.

"I'm going to come in your mouth. Swallow it all," Trevor said, his body going rigid as he shoved his cock deeper.

"Stacy," Trevor cried, his come filling her mouth.

The woman swallowed every drop before she tossed her head back and forth, moaning while Luis continued to give her pleasure. He wanted to hear his name from those luscious lips. Something about this woman had drawn him like a moth to a flame. And now, here she was in his bed and he wanted to reward her for taking the chance on him and Trevor.

"Luis, please," she cried.

"Come for me, baby," he said. "Come."

Trevor leaned over and sucked her breast into his mouth, chewing on her nipple, and she gasped.

Her body tightened and she flooded his tongue with her sweet nectar as she screamed his name, thrashing about on the bed. Naked, blindfolded, and moaning.

"Luis," she screamed.

"That's it, baby. We've got you."

A rippled shuddered through her body and he couldn't help but smile.

Rising, he nodded at Trevor. Time for the fun.

He'd laid out all their toys on the bed. He handed Luis the vibrator and he picked up a flogger.

With a sigh, she stretched her legs. "Are you going to fuck me now?"

He laughed. "Not yet, darling. We have more in store for you."

"What?"

"Spread your legs," he said.

Trevor took the flogger and ran it down her body, starting at her neck, trailing it over her breasts and down her stomach toward her womanly center.

"Oh," she said gasping.

When he trailed it over her clit, she tried to bring her legs together.

"Keep your legs open, or I'll tie you to the bed," he warned.

She moaned. "You're scaring me. I can't see," she said.

He ran his hand over her white buttocks, caressing her.

"Trust me, darling, it's going to feel good. We would never hurt you. Only give you pleasure."

Trevor raised the flogger and the strings landed on her clit.

"Oh," she cried.

"Did it hurt?"

"No," she gasped, instinctively drawing her legs together.

He hit her there again and she moaned and half rolled to her side. Trailing the flogger down her legs, he raised it again and it landed right on her pussy and she drew her legs up as if to cover herself.

Luis took out the strands of rope they had just for this and quickly tied her legs to the bed pedestals.

"Darling, I warned you," he said. Then he grabbed her arms and tied them as well. Now, she was spread eagle on their big bed. Wide open for them to do as they pleased.

"Luis," she cried. "Trevor. Please don't hurt me."

"We're not," Trevor said as he let the flogger's leather strings trail over her body. "Do you feel any pain? Or do you feel pleasure?"

She whimpered and he took the vibrator and worked over her clit that was now spread wide.

"Answer," Luis commanded.

"Yes," she gasped. "What you're doing feels so good."

"That's what we want to hear," Trevor said. He popped the flogger on her pussy.

"Oh," she cried.

"Pleasure or pain?" Trevor asked.

"Pleasure," she cried.

He popped her again and she lifted her hips off the bed.

Luis switched off the vibrator. Though he'd done this earlier, he wanted to taste her again, and again, and again.

With her spread wide, it was such a tempting sight, her pussy open, her clit gleaming with her juices.

Helpless and tied to his bed, she was such a tempting delight.

He held up his hand to motion for Trevor to stop. Leaning down, he kissed the inside of her thighs while Trevor moved up to her chest and trailed the flogger over her nipples. Luis moved to the inside of her legs, his lips trailing down her legs. Her pussy was wet, her clit was swollen.

Unable to resist, he ran his tongue up her leg and over her tortured clit before delving into her pussy. She smelled sweet and tasted even better.

"Oh," she cried. "You're torturing me?"

"Is it pleasure or pain?" Trevor asked.

"Oh, it's pleasure. Such pleasure."

Her hands gripped the coverlet on the bed and she raised her hips. Grabbing her buttocks, Luis lifted her pussy to his mouth and delved his tongue in as deep as it would go.

"Oh," she cried and struggled against the ropes.

"I'm going to come," she cried.

"Go ahead. Come for us now," Trevor said as he raised the flogger and caressed her breasts.

She screamed as the tendrils hit her nipples.

Her body rippled beneath his lips and Luis smacked her raised buttocks, the sound popping in the air.

That smack sent her over the edge as she cried out, her body shaking.

Rising, he smiled at Trevor. "I think she's ready."

Stacy's breathing was rapid and Trevor wanted to give her a chance to recover before they began again.

"Darling, are you ready for us to fuck you?"

She licked her lips. "Are you going to take me in the ass?"

"Not tonight," Trevor said. "But we can't wait to take you together, so that's in our plans eventually."

She licked her lips and swallowed.

"I'm ready," she whispered. "Please fuck me."

Luis went to her head and Trevor who had dropped the flogger, released her legs, but kept her blindfolded and her arms tied. Quickly, he opened a foil packet and sheathed himself.

"My cock is near bursting with need for you," he said as he lifted her hips and placed his penis at her entrance.

He rubbed his hard cock up and down her folds and she gasped.

"Do it," she cried. "I need you inside me."

"Your request is my command."

He shoved into her soaking wet pussy, his hard cock slamming inside.

"Oh," she cried. "You're huge."

"'That I am, darling, that I am," he said.

For a moment, they moved in unison as he held her hips, rocking her exactly like he wanted.

Reaching for her breasts, Luis twisted her nipples and she gasped. While he played with her breasts, he watched his friend push his fingers into her back passage.

"Trevor," she cried. "Luis."

She didn't know who was fucking her or playing with her ass.

"What, darling? Do you like my finger in your ass?"

"I…" she stammered.

"Be honest with us," he whispered against her head. "Or you'll be punished."

"Yes, it feels so good," she moaned. "Oh," she cried as he began to stretch her even farther with a second finger.

"Stacy, let me in. Soon we're going to take you back here," Trevor promised. "And I can't wait."

Luis couldn't wait either. But first, they had to prepare her.

"Aargh," she cried.

Luis covered her mouth with his as Trevor plunged three fingers into her and she moaned into his mouth.

She released Luis's mouth. "I'm going to come."

"Not yet. I'm not ready for us to come," Trevor said, and he slapped her ass.

"Trevor," she cried as she bit her lip. "Please."

Roughly he pounded her pussy, his cock slamming into her as Luis sucked on her nipples. She gripped the sheets and moaned, fighting to remain in control.

Another slap on the ass and Luis could tell she couldn't hold back much longer.

"Now, you can come," Trevor said.

She screamed with pleasure, her body shaking and undulating as the orgasm rocked her over and over while Luis held her.

Damn, he loved fucking like this. And it had been forever since his last time.

Trevor collapsed onto the bed.

They lay in silence as they all caught their breath. But it was hard to wait because Luis wanted to feel her pussy gripping his cock. He was hard as a rock and he'd been patient, but no more.

"Untie her arms. I want to roll her over and take her from behind," Luis said, reaching for the ropes. "Up on your knees, darling," he said as he rolled her to the side.

Slowly, she rose, the blindfold still covering her eyes.

Her pink rosebud was glistening with Trevor's cum as Luis lifted the smallest of the butt plugs and put lube on it. She was going to be surprised. He began to ease the dowel into her backside.

"What are you doing? I thought you said not tonight?"

"Darling, it's a butt plug. It's to prepare you for us to take you. It will stretch you so we don't hurt you."

He continued to corkscrew it into her little hole.

Once Luis had the butt plug in, he slapped her on the ass and then sheathed his cock. There would be no babies from this encounter. There would never be any babies.

Slowly he slid his cock into her pussy.

Pushing back, she wanted his cock and he gave it to her, knowing that he wouldn't last long. How could he when he'd been wanting this moment since the first time he saw her? Why did he have hope that this woman was the one who would help him overcome his nightmares and fulfill his dreams?

"No, it's too much," she groaned. "Take the plug out."

He was not going to take out the fullness that made her even tighter as she gripped his cock.

"Relax and it will be all right," Trevor told her while he twisted her nipples, pulling them into his mouth.

"Please hurry," she gasped. "I don't think I can hold off—"

Trevor plundered her mouth with his lips controlling her while his fingers twisted and pulled at her nipples.

Luis slapped her on the ass and she groaned.

"Stacy, come for me, now."

He raised her legs over her shoulders as he pounded into her pussy and then he smacked the butt plug.

A shudder rippled through them both. "Stacy."

"Luis," she screamed as she came all over his cock, her body shaking, with pleasure.

Releasing her legs, they fell to the bed, and he slumped over her, needing to catch his breath, needing to see what those sapphire eyes of hers would tell him.

He pulled the blindfold off and she stared at him with glassy eyes.

"Are you all right?"

A smile spread across her face. "A week. I get one week of this."

"Yes, one week," Trevor said.

But Luis wanted more. Already he liked this woman and he hoped that it would not be just a week but longer.

CHAPTER 3

Trevor woke before dawn even though he'd only had a couple hours of sleep. He'd always been an early riser, and he liked getting up, drinking coffee, and watching the sun rise. It was his time of the day when he sat and thanked the universe for taking care of him and the success he'd found in life. And for the billions he'd made with his company. For the land he loved that he and Luis shared.

For getting away from the family who hated him while he was growing up. Only his mother had really loved him. His father believed he was a freak and his brothers and sisters resented him for being so smart and the money he'd made.

Though he'd paid for their colleges and helped them get a good start in life, they were still extremely jealous of his success.

Why he'd received his high intelligence and not the others, he'd never understand, but he felt fortunate.

Being a bioscientist, he'd created a new beauty product guaranteed to make women's skin look younger and then he'd gone on to create a line of skin care that softened age. All in all, every one of his investors had made a lot of money. Including Luis.

It was what helped him and Luis afford this ranch. Here was his peaceful place. Where his mind often created new products. Where he dreamed of settling down with a woman and starting a family.

A family unlike his own.

But he and Luis were friends, and while the man might have acted family friendly, he really wasn't. And in many ways, Trevor couldn't blame him.

Once the sun came up, he went outside and fed the chickens. When he came back in, Luis was up, fixing breakfast.

"Good morning," he said. "Can't believe you got up so early. Not after a night like last night."

Trevor grinned. "Best night we've had in years. At first, I was skeptical of bringing Stacy home, but now I'm so damn glad we did."

Stacy was incredible and he really liked her. She was smart, funny, and so damn sexy, he didn't know how much he would be able to take.

Nodding, Luis pulled out a slab of bacon. "I think we're going to need protein to sustain us this week."

Sinking down at the kitchen table, Trevor shook his head.

"Did you really think it would be that good when she agreed to come home with us?"

The house had an old-fashioned kitchen that opened into a separate dining room. But there was a small breakfast nook where they could drink their morning coffee and look out at the pastures where the cattle roamed.

"No," Luis said as he put a slice of bacon in the pan.

"What do we do with her now?" Trevor asked. He didn't

have all week to spend in bed with her, though it was tempting. And he didn't want to train her for another two men.

He liked this woman and even wondered if she was the one he wanted to settle down with. Time would tell.

The smell of bacon wafted through the kitchen as Luis cooked.

"Today, I thought we would put her on the back of a horse and show her around the ranch. You've been wanting to ride out to the back pasture and check the fence."

Two weeks ago, he'd hired men to replace the back line with new barbwire. He wanted to check it out to make sure it met his standards. They didn't need their cattle roaming off down the highway.

"Good idea," he said. "Do you think she knows how to handle a horse? She's from New York City. There aren't many horses there for riding."

Luis chuckled. "Guess we'll find out. Damn, last night was good."

And it had been. Unless a woman was from Blessing, they often didn't take very kindly to the idea of two men at once. It had backfired on them before. While Stacy wasn't from around here, she'd seen her friend Kalie and knew what to expect.

"I was tempted to wake her up with sex again this morning. But I needed a break and I felt like maybe she did too. Not a long one, but a chance to recuperate."

A chuckle came from Luis. "Maybe a soak in the hot tub tonight."

"That sounds good," he said.

"When do you have to go back to Houston?"

"I've got an important meeting next week I'll have to be there for. What about you? What are your plans this week?"

Being the company boss was mighty nice. He could come and go as he pleased. Even Luis was free. The money they'd made when they were younger afforded them the lifestyle they wanted. A lifestyle that let them make their own hours.

"I'm meeting some of my old team members next week in Houston. I've got a family function Wednesday night. It's my mother's birthday, but other than that I'm free."

Trevor couldn't help but grin. "Your mother saw everything last night. You know she wants you to find a woman and settle down. She told me herself it was time you married."

Luis's family was one of the original settlers in Blessing. For generations, the men had shared a woman and wanted that for their grown children.

Luis flipped the bacon and laughed. "That's never going to happen. No woman should ever be saddled with me. It wouldn't be fair."

"Have you told your mother that?"

Before he became a Navy SEAL, they had talked of sharing a woman in marriage. But now, he wasn't certain that his friend wanted to marry any longer. At some point, they would have to make a decision about whether to continue or for Trevor to find another man who wanted to share a wife.

"She doesn't understand. She thinks all I have to do is be out of the military for a while and everything will be fine. I'll return to the boy who first joined the service."

"That's not going to happen," Trevor said. "We were both young and foolish, and I didn't even join the military."

"Instead you stayed behind and created a miracle cream for women."

Luis had dumped his entire trust fund into Trevor's creation, and when they'd launched the product, it had taken off. Now he was on the board of directors and they each received a hefty paycheck every month.

Without Luis's investment, he doubted the company would have made it.

A noise sounded on the stairs and they glanced toward the doorway that led into the kitchen.

"You think she's up?"

"Should be. It's after eight," Trevor said.

Luis chuckled. "But we wore her out last night."

Just then a sleepy-eyed Stacy appeared wearing Trevor's long-tailed white shirt. The tails hung down to her knees and she'd never looked sexier. Those long legs of hers were perfect for wrapping around a man's waist as he drove his cock into her.

"Good morning," she said with a yawn.

"Good morning, sleepy head," Luis said. "Come here."

She shuffled to the stove and he leaned down and kissed her softly on the lips. "I hope you're as tired as we are this morning."

"Yes," she said yawning. "I need coffee."

"Come here," Trevor said wanting to touch her silken flesh. It had been way too long since he'd run his fingers down her silky legs.

She slipped out of Luis's arms and walked to him. He pulled her down onto his lap, his hand running up the inside of her thigh.

His cock began to harden and he pulled her mouth down to his and kissed her. Even with morning breath, she tasted sweet. His hands moved to her bottom and he thumped the butt plug still in her ass.

Breaking the kiss, he slapped her on the ass. "We need to replace that butt plug this morning. It's time for another one. A bigger one."

A moan escaped her.

His fingers reached around the front of her and slid over her clit. "Oh my, you're wet. I should spread you right here on the table and do you again," he said. His fingers glided over her folds and he shoved a finger up her pussy. She gasped.

His hand reached beneath the shirt she wore and fondled her nipples.

"Tonight we're going to use nipple clamps on you." He breathed deeply off her neck and nipped along the side until he reached her shoulder. He shoved the shirt down until it fell in a puddle at her feet.

Turning her between his knees, his mouth found her nipple and he pulled it into his mouth. She pressed against him and he sucked on her hardened kernel. Even after last night, she tasted delicious and he wanted to continue what he'd started.

"I'm putting the eggs on," Luis said. "You started this. Finish her off."

"Gladly. Darling, it's your lucky morning," he said. "Lay across the table and spread your legs wide. Real wide. I'm going to have you before breakfast."

She did what he asked and he spread her open before he delved his tongue against her folds and she gasped. "Trevor."

"This week we're going to make certain that we fulfill your every wish. Your every desire, darling," Luis said while Trevor continued to work over her clit with his tongue.

"Oh," she cried, her body rippling with desire.

"Tell me what your desire is," Luis said as he flipped the eggs.

"I want both of you inside me at the same time," she gasped. "It's what I've dreamed about for years. Two men inside me at once."

"We're going slow, but you will get your desire," Luis said.

Trevor needed to make her come before their food grew cold. He pulled on the butt plug and then shoved it back in while his tongue created magic on her little love button.

She screamed as he continued to lave her clit with his tongue.

"Trevor, please," she cried. "I need to—"

"Come," Luis said. "Come now."

"Aargh," she cried when Trevor thumped on the plug, sending vibrations through her that he could feel with his tongue. With his teeth, he nipped her little bud and the effects were immediate.

A ripple went through her body and her pussy clenched on his tongue as her limbs shook.

She looked so beautiful and dazed as she came.

Trevor stood and nodded toward Luis.

"Now that's how you have breakfast."

Lying on the table, her chest rose and fell with her rapid breathing as she tried to gain control.

He picked up the shirt she'd been wearing and slipped it over her head and then he helped her rise from where they were going to eat.

When she was seated at the table, she leaned her head in her hand still looking disoriented.

"Darling, do you need me to feed you your eggs?" Luis asked.

With a sigh, she shook her head. "I've never experienced so much sex at one time. I may never be the same."

"As long as you're happy, we're doing our job," Trevor said as he wiped down the table with a cloth.

Luis handed her a plate with two eggs and several pieces of bacon. "Eat up. You're going to need your strength this week."

She turned her sapphire eyes and gazed at him, a smile on her face. "When I return to New York, where am I going to find two men like you boys who know how to treat a woman right?"

Maybe she didn't have to return. No, Luis didn't want to get married, but Trevor wanted a willing wife just like Stacy. One who would take them both at the same time. Only problem was Luis.

The man refused to even consider marriage, even though his family had done this for generations.

Maybe Stacy would be the woman to change his mind. Maybe there was hope that they could become another Blessing couple who shared a woman.

CHAPTER 4

Later, after Stacy had showered and put on jeans and a shirt, she came down the stairs. The men were waiting for her, their heads together. It was like they were plotting and she wasn't certain of what, but last night had been mind-blowing.

Never had she come so many times. Never had she enjoyed sex so much. And now, how would she ever experience this kind of gratification again in New York?

And then Trevor had started off this morning giving her another orgasm before breakfast.

Was this what Kalie, her friend, had experienced with her two cowboys? She didn't know for certain, but she'd seen the looks between her friend and her now-husbands. There was a sizzling tension between them that Stacy had been envious of. And now, here she was getting to experience her own two men.

Glancing around the house, she liked the modern updates they'd made to the ranch house. It had a cozy, warm feel about it. All it needed was a woman's touch, but she would only be here for a week. And then she had to return to New York.

"Have you ever ridden a horse?" Luis asked.

"Years ago when I was a kid at summer camp," she said.

Trevor smiled at her, and his look heated her. The way his golden-brown eyes seemed to skim down her body left her breathing fast and shallow. Of the two men, he was the most commanding in the bedroom, though Luis could become that way when she didn't do as he asked.

But Luis was the one who made certain she was all right, that she had everything she needed. Of the two, he was more caring and yet there was also a remoteness about him that she wanted to break through.

Right now, she was a little overwhelmed and knew that getting out would be good for them all. She wanted to learn more about these two attractive men who she'd been immediately drawn to. After one look from them, she'd wanted to remove her clothes. One look and she wanted to drop to her knees and take their cocks into her mouth. Never had she ever experienced this feeling of wanting.

And one kiss and she'd been begging them to fuck her.

"What are we doing?" she asked.

"We need to ride out to the back pasture and check the fencing. Trevor made a picnic lunch while you were showering and we want you to ride with us. Are you comfortable getting on a horse again?"

She licked her lips nervously and then she gazed at her men. This week was her only time with them, and she didn't want to sit in the house waiting. Wherever they went, she wanted to be right there at their sides.

"Will you help me?"

"Of course," Luis replied.

"It's been years," she said.

"We will give you the gentlest horse on the ranch. And we'll be right at your side," Trevor replied. "We're not going to let you get hurt."

Sighing, she nodded. "Let's go."

Luis gave her a cowboy hat and placed it on her head. "To keep the sun off of your face. We don't want that gorgeous skin of yours to turn red."

The men she dated in New York were nice young men, but none of them took care of her like these two guys. And she liked being treated like she was a piece of glass that would shatter if they didn't watch over her. It was nice to be treated so wonderfully.

Never had she met a man like either of them in New York.

Walking out the door of the house, she realized she hadn't seen their land in the daylight. It would be nice to be outdoors.

"This is beautiful," she said.

"Thanks," Luis replied. "Trevor sent me photos while I was overseas and told me this was our place. Once I saw the photos, I agreed."

Trevor grinned. The relationship between these two men was closer than brothers. And yet, last night while they were having sex, they never touched one another. At first, she'd been worried they might be bi-sexual, but they were strictly heterosexual.

Their focus had been on her. Yes, they each had their own orgasm, but their goal had been her pleasure. And she had loved every minute. Even the butt plug had been a hot experience she'd never imagined.

She followed them into a large barn. Inside the stalls were five horses. One by one, they led three outside and began the process of saddling them. The others, Trevor let out into the pasture.

"Those two are still very young and need more training," Luis said. "But Ginger, she's an older mare who is gentle and you just need to let her have some rein and she'll go anywhere you lead her."

A spiral of tension filled Stacy. It had been so long since she rode. She'd been a child filled with wonder.

"Here, give her a rub and talk to her," Trevor said, walking over to the beautiful red mare. "You'll soon be friends."

Taking his advice, she glided her palm along the muscled neck and the animal glanced at her with curiosity in her gaze. "I'm a newbie, Ginger, so please forgive me if I pull too hard or get nervous."

The horse gave a snort.

Once she was saddled, Luis handed her the reins.

"Stay right here and continue getting to know her while I saddle my horse and Trevor gets his ready to go," he said.

She patted the horse and rubbed her neck, continuing to talk to her. "Let's have a nice ride today. I'm only here this week and I really would like to learn more about what it's like living in this small town that I'm learning has quite the reputation."

When the men were finished, Luis came to her side. "I'm going to show you how to get on a horse."

It looked fairly easy and she had done it before, but she had been much more limber in those younger years. She did exactly like he showed her to put her right leg in the stirrup and swing over her left. Once she was up in the saddle, she held on tightly to the reins and leaned down.

"Thank you for standing still, Ginger," she said.

"Don't pull hard on the reins or she'll stand up and that's when you get into trouble. When you want her to slow down, pull back easy," he said. "We'll be on either side of you. Try to relax and let your body sway with the motion of the horse."

"All right," she said, sitting tall in the saddle trying to get accustomed to the feel of a horse between her legs.

"Let's go," Trevor said.

"Kick her sides gently," Luis said. "Give her a little slack in the reins and she'll be happy to keep up with the other horses."

The gentle red mare did exactly like he promised and soon they were riding out across the prairie. There were few trees in sight. Some oaks were in the distance, but mainly it was bare grassland with cattle dotting the landscape.

They rode along in silence and soon she began to relax.

"How long have you owned this property?" she asked.

"About five years," Trevor replied. "Luis was still in the Navy."

That was news to her. She didn't know he'd ever been in the military.

"You were in the Navy?" she said.

"Yes, I was a SEAL," he replied and she could tell he really didn't like to talk about it, but it explained so much about him. Those burly arms and the strength she'd felt when he held her.

Most military men were honorable and she could see that in Luis.

"Why did you go into the military?" she asked, wondering what made someone choose that kind of career and life.

Her body swayed in the saddle, the horse meandering alongside the other two animals.

A frown crossed Luis's face and she could see the tension in his body.

"Bad breakup in college," he said. "Plus, I didn't want to work for my family. So I went into the Navy thinking that would be easier. It never was easy, and after five years, I'd had enough."

She nodded, making a mental note that he really didn't like talking about his past, but she was curious about what made him into the man he was today. And she really enjoyed Luis. That little sprinkling of gray in his sideburns, the way his emerald eyes were large, dark, and intense sent a sparkle of pure heat through her even today.

"What about you, Trevor? Why did you want to buy this ranch?"

Trevor seemed more at ease as they rode.

"I'm a bioscientist," he said. "I like to study diseases and test different things. One day, I was working on a skin cancer cure. What I created didn't cure cancer, but it smoothed out older women's skin. It worked great on making skin look younger. So I took my formula and created a skin care company. Luis helped me with the funding and that's how I went from a scientist to a skin care company entrepreneur."

He had told her the name of his company and she'd been shocked. The company was worth billions, and while she'd never used the product, she liked the man who created the beauty line.

It was obvious that Trevor had an above-average intelligence. One man was brawny, and one was brainy. It was a perfect combination. And they were such good friends that it was a very nice arrangement.

Cattle watched them from the distance and one of them mooed a hello.

"How many acres do you own," she asked, gazing out at the land.

"A thousand acres," Luis replied. "We're running cattle on about five hundred of those acres and in the spring we'll divide the herd."

She just couldn't imagine that large of a spread. Not after living in New York City most of her life. Her apartment was less than a thousand square feet and was considered large compared to other living spaces in her price range.

The noise and the hustle and bustle were so different from what she was seeing out here on their land. It was such a different lifestyle.

It took them an hour to reach the fence that Trevor wanted to check and find that their workers had fixed it properly.

A line of oak trees separated the fence and the road and when they reached the area, Trevor pulled his horse to a stop.

When he swung his leg over his horse, she knew they were going to stop for a while and she was glad. Her butt was getting tired of bouncing in the saddle, though the horse had been good to her.

Luis helped her down, his hands wrapping around her waist as he held her while she slid down.

She reached up and patted Ginger on the neck. "Thank you for the nice ride. Now while we eat, you should munch on some grass."

The horse snickered.

"I think she likes you," Luis said, his arms around her. She leaned back into his chest and loved the way his body felt against her own. The smell of him even with the scent of horse and leather mixed in.

"Come on, you two. We need to eat," Trevor said.

He nuzzled her neck. "He's just jealous, and this morning I had to watch him going down on you while I fixed breakfast. He can wait."

She giggled. Being with these two men felt right. Already she knew their week together wouldn't last nearly long enough.

Would they visit her in New York? Doubtful, but she was going to ask.

Taking his hand, she pulled him toward the blanket Trevor had spread on the ground. He reached into his saddle bags and pulled out sandwiches, a bag of chips, and bottled water.

"Eat up," he said. "You're going to need the food."

She really wasn't hungry, but she sat on the blanket and unwrapped her sandwich.

"It's so quiet here," she said. "I love that the only noises are the birds and the cattle."

Trevor nodded. "It's why I hate going back to Houston. It's just so peaceful here."

"How often do you go back?" she asked.

"A couple of times a month for meetings," he said. "I have a small laboratory here at the ranch I often work in. I'll show it to you before you leave. You can even sample my newest creation. A lotion that has just the right amount of sunscreen in it that doesn't turn you orange."

Luis lay back with his legs crossed at the ankle, gazing at her. "Did you grow up in New York?"

With a sigh, she thought of her family. "Yes."

"Do you like it?"

It was hard to answer that question. It was all she'd ever known.

"Yes and no," she said. "This is so peaceful and yet what's left of my family is back there."

A frown crossed Trevor's face. "What do you mean *what's left of your family?*"

She hated talking about her father. It had been so many years ago and she barely even remembered him, though her mother once had photos of him everywhere in their home, but she'd died a year ago of cancer. Now she was alone except for some aunts and uncles.

Stacy was an only child because of what her father had done. And to the day she died, she'd both love and hate her father. It had been a weird thing to grow up without a father who was considered a hero and yet her mother resented him. She should have had brothers and sisters.

Her mother never forgave him. And Stacy still wasn't certain what to believe.

"My father died in the Twin Towers on 9/11," she said. "I was only three years old. So no, I don't remember much about him."

The men looked shocked for a moment.

"And this is why I never mention it," she said. "I never got the chance to really know my father."

Trevor cursed and Luis looked away.

"That's one of the reasons I became a Navy SEAL," he said. "Stopping assholes who want to harm Americans."

She sighed. "Do I wish I could have known my father? Of course, but I'm not going to let that day ruin my life. It ruined way too many lives and I'm just a small piece that was affected by what happened. I like to think my father would have wanted me to live my life in a positive way. And that's what I try to do."

Though she wished she would have had the chance to speak to him and confirm if what her mother told her was the truth.

There was silence for a moment as they finished their food and then Stacy lay back on the blanket. "You know, with the sun shining down on us, I could very easily take a nap."

"No," Trevor said, stood, and went to his saddle bags.

"I thought it might be fun to play outdoors. Off with your clothes," he said.

Glancing up at him, she stared at him. Was he crazy? What if someone saw them? Then she glanced around. There was no one for miles. He would laugh at her if she brought that up.

With a sigh, she sat up and removed her boots. Then she unbuttoned her blouse. Standing, she slowly unhooked her jeans and slid the zipper down. Glancing up, she noticed she had the attention of both men.

Shaking her hips, she bent over and slowly pushed down her jeans. When they reached her ankles, she looked at them between her legs. Both men were staring at her ass. She gave it a little wiggle.

"Stacy," Luis said, "you keep that up and I'm going to spank that voluptuous butt of yours."

She shook it again and he grabbed her. The next thing she knew her panties were ripped from her as he laid her over his knee.

"Count," he said.

"Don't hurt me," she cried, suddenly alarmed at what she'd done.

He gave a laugh. "Darling, I'm not going to hurt you. You're going to be begging me to fuck you before we're done."

Stacy swallowed hard and prepared for her first spanking.

CHAPTER 5

*L*uis had watched her ass swaying as she removed her jeans and couldn't wait to put his hands on her bare cheeks and spank her. The feel of her smooth ass as he slapped her cheeks was something he enjoyed.

Watching her skin turn from white to pink was a pleasure that he relished and he hoped she would as well.

"Darling," he said, rubbing his hands over her flesh, the butt plug peeking out at him as much an excitement as feeling her skin. "There is nothing more that a man enjoys from a woman than turning her gorgeous white cheeks pink. Tell me if I hit you too hard, but I really think you're going to enjoy this."

Trevor began to remove his clothes and Luis knew she'd soon be sucking his cock.

"Are you ready?" he asked her. "I can't wait to make your cheeks rosy."

Stacy still had her shirt and bra on, but the jeans were gone. He unhooked her bra and Trevor removed her shirt and lacy undergarment, leaving her naked. Nothing like baring a woman in the outdoors. It made Luis feel like he was Tarzan and she was Jane, and they were stranded in the jungle.

A bird flew over them and the breeze cooled him just a little, but not enough. Watching her slowly undress had made him ache to feel her rounded buttocks beneath his hand.

Caressing her ass, he let his finger slide down to her pussy.

"You're wet," he said. "I'm going to fuck you hard."

She whimpered.

"After I spank that pretty white ass of yours," he said.

"Don't hurt me," she gasped.

"Never. Now count your licks," Luis commanded as he raised his palm and brought it down to her flesh.

She gasped.

"One," she said. "How many are you going to give me?"

"Until I feel you've had enough for teasing me."

"But you enjoyed it," she replied.

He chuckled. "You're damn right I did. But I also like spanking you. It brings me pleasure."

Smack, his palm hit her flesh again.

"Two," she said, her voice shaking.

Smack, and this time his hand stung from the force of the blow.

"Three." She moaned, biting her lip. "That one was hard."

"Too hard?" he asked.

"No, but it stung."

His fingers delved into her pussy and she was now soaking wet. It wasn't too hard but enough that she noticed. Maybe that was the right combination to bring her pleasure.

"Darling, you're soaking wet. I think you like being spanked," he said.

"I like you being in control," she said with a gasp. "I like the way you're so damn strong and rugged. I like the way you make me feel."

No woman had ever admitted that to him, and he loved that Stacy was the one saying these things to him. She liked him being in control. He would have to remember that and use it later when he strung her up on the St. Andrews cross.

"Darling, you're going to get more licks for making me feel so good," he said.

Smack, the sound reverberated through the outdoors and she cried out, her butt wiggling on his lap like she wanted to escape.

"Four."

"Are you all right?"

"Yes," she said with a gasp. "It stings, but it also feels warm. Please, I need you to stick your fingers in me."

Trevor reached over and massaged her cheeks. "Time to suck my cock, Stacy."

She opened her mouth and Trevor slid his cock between her cheeks. She moaned around him as Luis let his fingers trail over her clit, rubbing the little nub.

"Oh, darling, keep doing that and I'll be shooting my load down your throat in no time."

"Ready for more?" he asked.

She nodded and he smacked her cheeks in rapid succession. A groan came from her.

"How can she count with your dick in her mouth," he said, glancing up at his friend. "Besides, I think it's my turn to have her suck my cock. You're always sticking your cock in there."

Trevor smiled. "You were busy doing what you love and I'm getting what I want. It's a win-win for all of us. Now finish our girl, so we can play with that gorgeous pussy of hers."

He was right. It was time to shove his cock so far in her that she would think it was coming out her throat.

Smacking her on the ass, he hit her several more times, causing her to gasp.

"Darling, I've enjoyed this so much, but I can't wait to stick my cock in you again."

Just then Trevor grabbed her face and held her head as he used her mouth to reach his climax.

With one last shove, he sighed and fell back.

"You don't know what you're missing," he said as he smiled at Luis.

She swallowed and then wiped her mouth.

"Oh, I'll find out soon," he said.

Laying Stacy out on the blanket, he stood and removed his clothes.

"I can't wait to fuck you," he said.

Luis quickly shed his jeans and shirt. His cock sprang out of his boxers ready for action. Leaning down onto the blanket, he slipped his fingers between her legs and pulled them apart, letting his fingers trail over her clit. "While you're here this week, we'll spank you with pleasure and for punishment. Do you understand? Anytime you disobey, you'll get a punishment spanking. When you obey, I'll make that ass of yours sing with pleasure."

"Yes," she cried out.

"Up on your knees," he said. "I want to take you from behind."

It was his favorite position. Not that he wasn't willing to try any position she wanted. As long as he was in control.

"Are you going to play with the butt plug," she asked as she moved onto her knees and looked over her shoulder at him.

There was something about that innocent expression on her face that made him want to train her, teach her, and have her experience everything that he loved. Never had he wanted to do this with a woman, but Stacy was an exception.

"Yes, why?" he asked.

"Because I like it when you do that," she said with a gasp as he thumped the plug on the end.

"Time for a bigger one," he said, pulling it almost out and then shoving it back in. She gasped and cried out.

"More," she said. "Please more."

Pulling the butt plug almost all the way out, he shoved it back in and then thumped it with his finger, feeling it vibrate.

A moan escaped her as she leaned on her front arms, her ass high in the air.

Trevor moved her over the top of him and he slid down until his mouth was on her nipples.

"Darling, it's time for me to put my cock inside you," he said, unable to wait any longer. Quickly he pulled out the foil packet from his jeans and sheathed his cock. Never would he have unprotected sex because the consequences would be dire.

He thrust his fingers into her pussy and she moaned. Soon he intended to have her screaming his name with passion. Spreading her cheeks, he put his mouth against her pussy and she pushed back giving his mouth more access.

Unable to wait any longer, Luis moved behind her. She leaned back, glanced at him, and licked her lips. It was such an enticing expression and he couldn't resist her any longer.

Eager to feel his cock constricted, he slammed into her

pussy. A groan escaped from her as her body stretched, and he filled her with his dick. She moved her hips to accommodate him, and for a moment, they moved in unison as he held her, rocking her exactly like he wanted.

She clung to his cock and moaned and sighed. While he fucked her, Trevor twisted her nipples and sucked her breasts.

But that wasn't all he wanted.

His fingers slid up to her back passage and he tapped the butt plug with his finger before he pulled it out and then shoved it back in. She gasped.

Luis moaned. He couldn't wait to get his cock inside that sweet little hole. And she seemed almost as eager.

"Oh," she cried as he twisted the plug inside her. "Do that again. Please take me there."

"Soon, baby, soon," he moaned. "I'm going to enjoy taking you with Trevor. I'm going to love shoving my big cock up your tight little hole while Trevor bangs your pussy and then we'll switch."

Trevor reached for her nipples and twisted them. "Soon you're going to take our cocks at the same time. We'll fuck you all night long together."

"Oh, please may I come, please?" she cried.

Trevor's lips covered hers and Luis could feel his come starting to build as he plunged into her pussy over and over. The tight walls of her gripping him, massaging him, bringing him right to the edge.

She released Trevor's mouth. "I'm going to come."

"Not yet, you're not," Luis said, and he slapped her ass, but this time between the two of them, it was pure pleasure.

"Luis," she cried as she bit her lip. "Please."

Shoving the plug in her, he twisted it one more time.

Between the thin wall of her ass and her pussy, the butt plug kept her nice and tight just like when he and Trevor would share her. Just thinking about it was driving him closer to the edge, spinning him out of control.

"Now, you can come," he said as he slammed his cock into her one last time, his seed spilled into the rubber.

She screamed with pleasure, her body shaking and undulating as the orgasm rocked her over and over.

Luis and Stacy collapsed onto the blanket. The two men moved her until she was between them in the warm Texas sun. They needed her close.

They lay in silence as all three tried to catch their breath. A butterfly buzzed above them searching for a sweet flower.

What was it about this woman? Never had he thought of training a woman to make him happy. Marriage was out of the question due to his time in the Navy, but if he could, it would be with Stacy.

"Now, for your next butt plug," Trevor said, rising from the blanket and going to his saddle bags.

"Up on your knees," Trevor demanded.

"But I'll be riding Ginger home and those butt plugs take a while to get adjusted."

"Who said we were done?" Luis said.

"Oh," she said. "It's just the sun is starting to sink and you promised me we could get in the hot tub tonight."

"And we will," he said, running his hand down her hair. "But first, you're getting another butt plug."

Slowly, she turned over and crawled onto her knees. He pushed her head down until her ass was in the air just like they wanted. Luis watched as Trevor's fingers stroked her clit and pushed into her pussy.

"Oh, Trevor," she moaned, "make me come."

"Not yet. The best is yet to come," he said and slapped her pussy.

A scream tore from her throat. Not one in pain, but pure pleasure. "Oh, do that again."

And he did.

Spreading her thighs, Luis exposed her back passage, her little rosebud hugging the plug in place. Slowly he removed the smaller plug while he pushed the lubrication into her ass, his fingers spreading and stroking her little pucker while she groaned.

"Get on with it, man. I want to fuck her," Trevor said.

Slowly Luis pushed the third butt plug into her.

"All in," Luis said and gave her a smack on the ass.

She yelped, but it sounded more like a moan.

"On your back and spread your legs," Trevor commanded.

Stacy stared at him with desire-glazed eyes. "Trevor, please. I need you inside me."

Trevor took his time as he pushed into her pussy and she groaned.

"Damn, she feels even tighter," he said as he began to burrow into her pussy, raising her hips to meet his thrusts.

Luis sank down beside her and twisted her nipples before he leaned in to kiss her, his mouth ravaging hers. He demanded that she surrender under the assault of his lips and she groaned.

She was helpless. They were her masters and she was all theirs to do with as they wished. And Luis had always liked his sex a little rough. With Stacy, he wanted to push her to the very brink before he soothed the maelstrom he created. With

Stacy, he didn't want to think of tomorrow, just enjoy the moment and pray that his demons stayed away.

"Oh," she cried into Luis's mouth as his tongue ravished her. He broke the kiss and she screamed, "Please, Trevor, let me come."

Trevor raised her legs over her shoulders as he pounded into her pussy and then he smacked the butt plug.

"Now you can come," he said as he sent vibrations through her again.

The smack was hard enough that even Luis could feel it through her lips.

"Trevor," she screamed as Luis gathered her in his arms and she disintegrated. This was the life he'd always dreamed of until the Navy took that from him.

CHAPTER 6

That night, Trevor's cell phone refused to stop buzzing. He'd put it on vibrate, hoping to have this week to spend with Stacy. Right now, he didn't want to deal with anything except her sweet pussy.

Especially not his family. Not even work. But maybe something had happened and he needed to find out.

They were sitting in the hot tub, relaxing and watching the moon rise in the clear night sky. It had been a fabulous day, and tonight, he would once again be between her legs.

The woman would soon be taking them both at the same time and he dreamed of that moment. At the same time, they would claim her and he hoped they would make her theirs permanently. But that depended on Luis.

Finally, after hearing his phone repeatedly buzzing, he grew fearful. What if something had happened to his mother or his brothers and sisters? Or even his business. He needed to check and see who kept calling him.

"Excuse me while I find out what's wrong," he said, climbing out of the hot tub.

Grabbing a towel, he went into the house.

Glancing at his phone, he saw that it was his mother. What if someone was hurt?

Quickly he called her back. "Hi, Mom. What's so urgent."

"Your brother Diego has flunked out of college," she said. "I thought you should know so you don't pay anything else to that school. I'm so angry with that boy. He's lazy."

Diego spent a lot of time getting into trouble. This wasn't the first time he'd flunked a class. "Was it just one class or all of them?"

"All of them. He's not even bothering to attend any longer. He's not stupid, Trevor, he's just not into learning like you," she said. "I fear that he's going to get into trouble and find himself in jail."

With the kids that Diego hung with, that could soon be an option. But it was his choice.

Trevor had paid for all of his siblings to go to school. His brother Antonio had done well, and one sister had graduated, while the other was close, but Diego wanted him just to give him money each month and forget about education. That's not how it was going to work.

And with this news, Trevor knew it was time to cut him loose. Yes, he would be considered the bad brother. Diego would call him all kinds of names and say that he was selfish, but he didn't care.

He'd given them each an opportunity he didn't have and yet Diego didn't see it that way. He just wanted a handout. Trevor had given up so much to graduate from college and to make his company successful. His brother had been given a helping hand. What he did with that was his choice.

"Mother, let him be. If he wants to quit, I'm not going to

stop him. It's his life. His choice and if he wants to remain poor, that's his decision. But I'm no longer paying for his education unless he wants to return full-time, and even then, it will not be an unlimited check. Let him be. Let him show us if he has any ambition. Time for him to decide what he wants in life."

His mother started crying. "Why didn't I have more sons like you?"

He'd paid off his mother's house, set her up with a monthly allowance, and even bought her a new car. She'd worked for years to make certain they had what they needed after his father had died.

The father who did nothing but make fun of him. Who ridiculed him because he was so smart.

"Momma, stop crying. It's time for Diego to choose his path. We can no longer help him," he said.

"Son, promise me you're going to find a beautiful, smart, young woman and settle down. I want to hold your babies before I die," she said, sniffling.

The image of Stacy came to mind and the thought of her belly swelling with his child filled him with warmth. But that wasn't what Luis wanted. And he'd only known her for several days. Time would decide if she was the one for him.

"When are you going to come see me?"

Two weeks ago when he went to Houston, he stopped by and visited her and the rest of his family. This was not the week he wanted to think about them. The thought of Stacy naked in the hot tub flashed in his head and he wanted to get off this phone as soon as possible. This was his week with her.

"Momma, I promise I'll come by soon. I've got to go. We have company and I want to get back to my guests," he said.

There was a moment of silence and then he heard the hopeful note in her voice. "Oh, you have company? A woman?"

"Goodnight, Momma. Let me know what Diego decides to do," he said. "And you can tell him no more money from me. Time for him to become a man."

She gave a giggle. "It must be a woman. You sound anxious."

"Goodnight, Momma," he said again.

"Goodnight, my son, bring her to meet me," she said. "Oh, I hope she's the one."

He disconnected the call and turned. Stacy stood in the doorway of the house.

"Sorry, I came in to get us more champagne," she said.

"No problem," he said. "That was my mother."

A smile spread across her face. "I could tell. Mothers can be very insistent sometimes."

"Yes," he said. "Plus, she was upset about my little brother Diego dropping out of college. I'm done with him. He's on his own."

She walked into the kitchen and he followed her.

"How many brothers and sisters do you have?" she asked.

"Two brothers and two sisters. There are five of us. We struggled when I was a child. No money and food was scarce. It was one of the reasons I knew I would be successful," he said taking the champagne bottle from her hands.

"Are you paying for your brothers and sisters to go to college?"

"Yes," he said. "It was the least I could do to help them."

So far only one of them had flunked out and that was Diego. But hopefully he would soon learn that not having a degree would not help him move up in this world. And no, he would not receive a monthly stipend to live on. Trevor wasn't a money tree.

He pulled her in close to his naked body.

"This is the kind of life I've always dreamed of having. But I'd love it even more if there was a woman between us all the time," he said.

He saw the confusion in her gaze.

"But I live in New York and you're here," she said, running her hand down his face. At her touch, his cock began to harden.

"I know," he said. "Let's just see how this week goes."

"Trevor," she said as he put the cold champagne bottle against her nipples, sending a ripple through her. "What is the divorce rate in Blessing?"

He laughed. "I'm not sure, but it's very low."

His fingers trailed down her naked body and he twisted one of her nipples that was ice cold from the champagne bottle.

"Come on," he said with a gasp. "If we don't get back out there, I'm going to be tempted to fuck you on the kitchen table again."

A grin spread across her face. "I think you gave me oral sex there this morning. That seems like a long time ago, maybe we should do it again."

Grabbing her hand, he pulled her out the door, knowing Luis would be getting suspicious with them gone for so long. And yes, he was tempted to take her right there on the table again, but this time he wanted more. He wanted to put his cock inside her and fuck her till she screamed his name.

They walked outside and she stepped up into the hot tub.

"Is everything all right?" Luis asked Trevor.

"Diego dropped out," he said. "Not my problem any longer."

His youngest brother had always been the favored one and his handsome looks and lazy nature were working against him. But Trevor wasn't going to think of his sibling when he had a beautiful woman he couldn't wait to fuck sitting beside him in the hot tub.

Luis nodded. "That boy needs to join the military and learn some discipline."

"It would be a good option for him," Trevor said. "But right now, I need to concentrate on this blonde beauty that's in our hot tub. She looks like she needs to be fucked."

A grin spread across her face. Rising to her knees, she turned her ass to him. "Trevor, you're so right. I need you."

She didn't have to ask him twice. Standing, he planted his feet and bent her over the edge of the hot tub. Then he shoved his cock into her hot willing pussy.

"I'm going to make you forget every man you've ever had sex with, but me and Luis. By the time I'm finished with you, no other man will satisfy you. We'll send you back to New York ruined for any other men."

Luis leaned back and smiled. He reached out and pulled her hand from the edge of the hot tub and wrapped it around his cock.

"I'm going to help him. When this week is over, we'll send you back to New York satisfied and unable to find anyone to ease the tension we've created inside you. No man, nothing will satisfy you. You'll come back to Blessing, begging us to fuck you."

Slamming into her, he pummeled her sweet channel and she squeezed his cock.

"Fuck me," she said. "How will I ever survive with just one lover? I'm going to need two big strong men to always satisfy my needs."

Trevor leaned against her back. "Especially after we both take you at the same time. You'll be ruined and you'll soon be coming back wanting us to do you again."

And already he didn't want to let her go. After only two days, he wanted to somehow tie themselves to her and keep her here by their side. But Luis was the problem. Since the Navy, his best friend claimed he would never marry and never have children, but Trevor wanted a family of his own.

Soon they would need to make a decision.

He removed the butt plug they had just put in this afternoon and rammed first one finger and then a second finger inside her ass. With his other hand, he reached around and found her clit. He twisted the little nub, causing her to groan even louder.

His finger and his cock began a dance as he shoved his finger into her little rosebud and shoved his cock inside her. Oh God, this woman was tying him in knots inside. How he wanted her to stay with them. Maybe even become their wife, but it had only been two days.

They still had at least four more days with her before she had to leave. Four more days to convince Luis that he did want to get married and for the three of them to live together.

"May I please come," she cried.

"No," he said, twisting his fingers in her ass. "Not until Luis comes. Then we'll both come."

Luis looked over at her. "Darling, this hot water is making

it difficult. Maybe you should lie on the deck and I'll be right beside you."

Shocked that his friend couldn't come in the hot tub, Trevor climbed out with them and spread out on the deck. Trevor watched as Luis picked up the bottle of champagne. He waited until Trevor was once again pounding her pussy before he lifted the bottle and poured the cold alcohol over her body.

She shuddered as he began to lick the champagne off her skin, dipping his tongue into her navel and over her breasts while she stroked him with her fingers.

Tensing, Luis came all over her, squirting his seed over her breasts and belly.

Gasping, she cried out. "Trevor. Please."

"Come for me, sweetheart," he said as he shoved his cock into her and exploded inside her sweet pussy.

They all collapsed onto the deck, their breathing heavy.

"What are we going to do tomorrow?" she asked laughing.

Luis smiled. "Fuck you senseless."

"Again and again," Trevor said, knowing that's all he wanted to do.

CHAPTER 7

The next day, they decided not to leave the ranch. Luis removed her clothes and when she stepped out of the shower, he let her dry off, but he gave her the news.

"You're to remain naked all day. This way, we can fuck you whenever we want," he said. "And, darling, we want to a lot."

Stunned, she stared at him. "Naked? What if someone stops by to visit you?"

"Then you'll go upstairs and wait," he said. "No clothes. Unless, of course, you want me to paddle your ass. And, darling, I would love to."

"You told me Trevor was the one who wanted to spank me. I think it was really you," she said, giving him a saucy look.

"You're right. I do. Because there is nothing like the sound of your sweet moans and the feel of your sweet wetness on my fingers after I'm done. Now, do you want to disobey me?"

Shaking her head, she gazed at this man she was finding she adored more each day. "Not yet. Maybe later. I'd like to be able to sit down some today."

A grin spread across his face. "I always knew you were a smart woman."

Tossing him a smile, she walked out of the bathroom into the bedroom.

Trevor was waiting for her. "Up on your knees. Time for another butt plug."

Good grief, she was getting tired of wearing these things up inside of her. "How many more are there?"

"One more and then we'll take you together."

At least, soon, she would not be enduring these any longer. Soon, they would give her what she'd desired for years, and she was ready to take them both at the same time. The thought of them both inside her was kind of scary, but it was her fantasy, and they had promised to fulfill her desires.

But this butt plug appeared different. It had batteries inside it.

"Wait a minute," she said. "Does this one vibrate?"

They didn't answer, which was not good. Crawling onto the bed, she got up on her knees and waited for Trevor to put lube in her ass before he greased up the latest plug.

It took him a few tries to get it in and she had to endure him tweaking her clit and slowly pushing it inside her.

"Darling, this one you're going to love," Luis said. crawling beneath her. His mouth covered her nipples as he sucked her breast into his mouth.

"I thought we were going to cook lunch," she said, gasping as Luis began to stroke her clit.

"We are," Trevor responded. "But first we have to get you prepared."

A tingle vibrated through her as he turned on the plug.

"Oh," she cried as her body began to buzz with the feel of

the plug inside her and Luis's fingers stroking her folds. "Trevor."

"Yes, darling," he said. "I knew you were going to love this one. And so are we."

Oh, her need climbed inside her. "I can't do this."

Trevor slapped her on the ass. "Yes, you can and you will."

They always pushed her and had her do things she didn't think she was capable of. But this vibrator was like someone deep inside her causing her to scream with pleasure.

"Darling, we're going to make you feel so good today," Luis replied.

They made her feel good all week, but at this moment, the vibrations were so much, and she didn't know if she could hold off the orgasm coming at her like a tsunami. Between the vibrations and Luis's fingers, she was so close to exploding.

And then she heard Trevor unzipping his jeans and them sliding to the floor.

The ripping of a foil packet let her know he was soon going to be inside her.

"Hurry," she cried, needing something to fill her pussy. Something to make this urgent need go away. "I'm not going to last much longer."

A chuckle came from him. "Don't worry, darling. I'm not either. Just the look of that vibrator inside your ass, causing it to jiggle, is more than enough to push me to the edge. And the feel of it," he sighed. "Dear God, Luis, where did you find this monster?"

"I'll never tell," he said. "But I bought it overseas."

He pulled her mouth to his, his lips demanding surrender and she gave in to his control. Wanting him, needing both of them. In the three days she'd been here, they had controlled her body in ways she'd never dreamed of. Ways she didn't know she needed.

And this morning, she'd planned on cooking them a really nice lunch and dinner, but instead, she was once again on her knees letting them take her to the brink of oblivion.

"May I come?" she cried, not able to hold back much longer.

Trevor slammed into her and slapped her on the ass.

"Now," he cried. "Come for me now."

A scream tore from her throat as the butt plug vibrated deep inside her and Trevor came as they both pulsated. All she cared about was the feelings these two men invoked in her.

Luis's kiss was deep and controlling, and as she came, she moaned into his mouth. He pulled away from her lips and gazed at her. The buzzing stopped and she collapsed onto the bed with Trevor crawling next to her.

"What did you think? Should we do it again?"

"Not yet," she gasped, knowing this vibrator could send her over the edge so fast, especially with one of them deep in her pussy.

Lying beside them, she realized that with each passing day, her heart was becoming involved and that frightened her. What had started out as just two men showing her about how life existed in Blessing was now becoming something she didn't want to give up.

All her life, she'd wanted a close-knit family. She wanted a husband and children and everything that was important in this little town. This was why her friend Kalie had decided to stay here and marry her men.

And now Stacy understood why. But she didn't even know how Luis and Trevor felt about marriage, family, and children. And her own large family was a dream she was not willing to sacrifice for any man. No matter how well they treated her.

What was she doing? This week was supposed to be just about sex, and suddenly she was trying to make it into something more.

With a sigh, she lay there on the bed.

She didn't say a word, needing time to reflect on her growing feelings. They all had agreed to no commitments. Just a week of sex. A week of them teaching her about life in Blessing. A week of fulfilling her desires and fantasies.

"I'm starving," Trevor said, sitting up on the bed, naked.

"You should be," Luis said. "You're the one who got to come."

"So did Stacy," Trevor replied.

"This week is about her. She should come as many times as we can make her," Luis said. "But you're right. I'm starving as well. Let's cook some lunch."

The two men jumped up from the bed and then they glanced down at her.

"You all right?" Trevor asked.

"I'm fine," she replied, knowing that she really wasn't. "I'll be right down. I want to clean up first."

"No clothes," Luis said.

She'd agreed to being naked.

"We'll get started on lunch," Trevor replied.

"I'm making dinner," she said.

They nodded and walked out.

It was the first time they had really left her alone and she curled into a ball. What was she doing? Maybe she should pack her bags and leave. Because already, she could feel herself falling for these two men. And they all promised no attachments.

And yet, she loved being with them. They were so good to her. So kind, thoughtful, and they took care of her. They looked out for her and made certain she was getting what she desired.

Glancing around the bedroom, she knew that it was going to be hard to leave on Saturday morning, but she had no choice. It would take her almost all day to fly back to New York and then on Monday, she had to show up to work.

Her life was in the Big Apple. Their lives were here in Texas, and there was a lot of country between them.

After crawling off the bed, she went into the bathroom and cleaned up. Tears were in her eyes and she quickly wiped them away. No tears. No regrets. No thinking of what-if.

While she was here, she was going to enjoy her time with her men. She had to live for today because tomorrow this would only be a memory.

Pasting a smile onto her face, she went downstairs. In the kitchen, she was surprised to see Luis was alone.

"Where's Trevor?"

He shook his head. "He had to run out to the lab and give the main office some numbers from his last experiment. Something about they didn't get the same results as he had. He's a freaking genius and he gets quite upset when someone botches his inventions or doesn't do what he tells them."

She gave a chuckle. She could see that in a man like Trevor. The man was so damn intelligent.

"What do you want me to do to help?"

"Nothing," he said. "You get started on the dinner you want

to make us. I'm going to fix us a late brunch and then we'll be good until tonight."

"I need a large kettle pot," she said.

He reached into the cabinet and handed one to her, but somehow when they went to transfer it from his hands to hers, she dropped it.

The pan clattered onto the tile floor, the sound loud and ringing throughout the room.

Reaching down to pick it up, she heard a strange noise. It was almost like a strangled cry. Standing, she whirled around to see Luis in a crouched position, his hands over his head.

"Get down," he screamed. "Incoming. Get me the damn command base on the radio transmitter. They've got us pinned down. Tell them to send in helicopters. Now, damn it, now."

She reached over and ran her hand down his arm. "Luis, it's Stacy. You're here. You're home."

"The fuck I am," he cried. "Get down, soldier, or you're going to die. John help save this rookie."

She crouched down beside him, not knowing what to do. "You're home in Texas. You're safe. You're on the ranch with me and Trevor."

His emerald eyes were glazed as they stared at her. His body was tense and she could tell he was in that horrible place where his life was in danger. How did she bring him home?

"Luis, come back to me," she said, not knowing what to do or say, only that she needed him to be all right. "Luis."

She raised her voice somehow hoping that would penetrate his delusion.

Just then the back door opened and Trevor walked in.

"Shit," he cried when he realized what was going on. "Help me get him up."

They tried to help Luis stand, but he fought them off. "Stay down, soldier, unless you want to die. Incoming."

He fell flat on the floor, covering his head with his hands, his body was shaking.

Maybe it was the cold tile. Maybe it was the smell of bacon frying, but somehow he jerked and then crawled into a fetal position before he glanced up at them.

Slowly, she could see him returning, and she also saw fear in his eyes. What had this man lived through that brought this on?

"What the hell happened?"

Trevor tried his best to act like it was nothing. "Just a little piece of the war came to visit you today."

With a sigh, Luis sat up on the floor. "What did I say?"

"Just the usual stuff. Incoming, get down, soldier," Trevor said. "If you're going to do this, I wish you'd spill some military secrets."

Luis jerked and then shook his head. "No, you don't want to know. It would scare the hell out of you."

He gazed at Stacy. "Sorry, you had to witness that."

"No, it was my fault," she said. "I dropped the pan you gave me and it seemed to trigger you."

Getting to his feet, he shook his head. "They keep telling me I'll get over this, but I'm not sure. Any kind of loud noise can trigger it. Damn military."

Stacy walked over to him. "Don't. You served your country. Don't be ashamed that you have episodes where you go back into the fighting. What I saw was a man who was frightened for his life and his soldiers' lives. I think that's honorable."

Luis shook his head. "It makes me feel so damn weak that I can't control it. Why is my brain doing this to me?"

Grabbing his arm, she tried to pull him to her, but he refused.

"Weak? You're one of the strongest men I've ever met," Stacy said. "You're an ex-Navy SEAL. They don't get much stronger than that."

"But the battle I always go back to is the one where a good friend died. I should have saved him."

"No," Stacy said. "I'm certain you did everything you could to protect him."

"But it wasn't enough," he said. Looking forlorn, he sighed. "If you guys don't mind, I think I'll go upstairs and lie down for a little bit. Let me know when lunch is ready."

Stacy watched as he walked out the door and up the stairs.

"Did I say something wrong?" she asked Trevor.

"No, but when this happens it leaves him weak as a kitten. He'll probably sleep for a couple of hours. It will be good for him."

Standing there naked, she felt so forlorn. This was all her fault. If she hadn't dropped the damn pan, he would not have returned to battle.

"I didn't know about his friend," she said.

"Some things, no matter how long ago it happened, you just don't get over. Luis has never forgiven himself for losing John."

Shaking her head, she felt bad for the big strong Navy SEAL. How did you get over losing a friend in battle? Maybe he never would.

CHAPTER 8

*L*uis had never been so embarrassed. Just when he thought the episodes were going away, one would surprise him at the worst possible moment. Why couldn't he put the war and the death of his best friend behind him?

When the relapses happened, the episodes left him weak, exhausted, and almost despondent. Now instead of trying to push through, he often lay down and rested. When he did, he seemed to come out of it faster.

Today, he'd slept three hours. He'd missed brunch with them and even the afternoon. When he awoke, he remembered that today was his mother's birthday and the family was throwing a big party for her later this evening.

And Stacy had cooked them dinner. Hopefully, she wouldn't mind them waiting to have it until tomorrow night.

Rushing down the stairs, he realized they had only an hour to dress and get over to his parents' house.

How would his family accept Stacy? They didn't know she was staying with them and yet, he couldn't not take her. He wasn't about to make her stay behind when he liked having her at his side.

"We've got to get dressed and go," he said, all but running into the room. They weren't there.

Picking up his phone he dialed Trevor's number.

"Where are you?"

"I'm showing Stacy my lab," he said.

"We've got to get ready to go. It's Mother's birthday and we're all expected at the house within the hour."

"All right. We'll be there," Trevor said. "Are you feeling better?"

"Yes," he said. "But I forgot today is Mom's birthday. I should've called her. I can't miss tonight."

Luis ran back up the stairs to change his clothes. The others came in.

"I'll stay here," Stacy said. "It's a family affair. We can have the casserole I made tomorrow night."

After his earlier episode, he wanted her by his side. He needed her close and he wanted her to be with his family.

"No, I want you to go with us," he said. "You've been around my family before. I need you by my side tonight."

He watched as concern filled her beautiful face. "But they all believe I left on Sunday. We said there would be no complications and what are they going to think?"

Trevor stepped up beside her and pulled her against his chest. "This is Blessing. People don't speculate about what's going on in someone else's house. You'll be with us. Don't worry about what people think. It's none of their concern."

Luis could see that she was still worried. "You're with me and Trevor. That's all anyone needs to know. Believe me, they won't ask questions, but my mother may be curious."

"You're certain you want me to go?" she said.

"Yes, I do," he said. "Being with people is what I need, and you're the one who excites me, so yes, please go with us."

He would have been all right if she wasn't there, but he really wanted her beside him. The time of her departure was fast approaching, and he wanted to spend as much time with her as he could. And he hoped and prayed that he would not have another episode. Sometimes he went weeks without one and then something would trigger him and he'd be back in the jungle having an episode every few days.

"All right," she said. "What should I wear?"

"Nothing formal. We'll all be in jeans, shirts, and boots."

Quickly they dressed and Stacy put on makeup. It was the first time since the wedding that she'd really dolled up and she looked stunning. His mother was going to be asking the questions tonight and he hoped he could convince her that it was just for a week.

"Damn," Trevor said. "You're beautiful."

"Thank you," she said. "All right, I'm ready. Let's go if you're certain."

Shaking his head, Luis took her hand and pulled her down the stairs and outside to his truck.

Thirty minutes later, they pulled up in the driveway. As soon as they arrived, Luis kissed his mother on the cheek. "Happy birthday, Mom."

She smiled at him. "I'm so glad you're here. And who did you bring with you?"

"You remember Stacy from the wedding," he said.

"You're Kalie's friend," she said. "You were the maid of honor at their wedding. I so hope they're having a good time on their honeymoon."

Stacy stepped up beside Luis. "Hello, Ms. Nash. Happy birthday."

His mother's smile widened. "Welcome. You're here with Luis and Trevor?"

"Yes, ma'am," she said blushing.

The woman's happiness spread across her face and she took Stacy by the arm and led her away from the men. Luis shook his head, knowing this was what he expected tonight. Following behind them, he heard his mother talking to Stacy.

"I have only one request. Please don't break my son's heart. He's been through so much and I want him to be happy."

Luis watched as his mother took Stacy away. He heard her words to her, but what could he say? They had agreed to no commitments, and while he was having second thoughts, Stacy's home was over a thousand miles away and after being separated from his family for so long while he was in the military, he wasn't going anywhere.

Plus, after today, she would never want a man like him. And he would never saddle a woman with his problems. No, his episodes didn't happen every day, but still, it wouldn't be fair for a woman to have to deal with his unexpected returns to the jungle.

He watched the two women's heads go together and they talked in hushed tones that he couldn't hear.

"Your mother is something else," Trevor said. "Look at the way she's stolen Stacy from us. She's probably filling her head with all kinds of things about you and me. How we were always the troublemakers in school. But more than anything, I bet she's trying to convince her to stay and marry us."

That was what Luis feared as well.

"I'm not a good catch," he said.

"I think we're both damn fine catches. And for her, I would stop running and lay down and let her catch me anytime, anywhere, any place."

Oh, how Luis wished it was that simple.

"But you don't suffer from PTSD," Luis said. "If you want to marry her, ask her. But I'm never getting married."

Trevor clenched his fist. He looked so frustrated.

"Now, how hard would that be? I'm married to her and bedding her and you're just going to stand there and watch? Besides, you should have seen her with you. She was genuinely concerned and she was trying to talk you out of where you were."

People around them were talking and laughing and Luis felt like an outsider. Here, at his own mother's birthday, he feared he would have a flashback and send everyone fleeing.

"But what if I hurt her? What if I thought she was the enemy and tried to kill her? What if I hit her? No, I can never marry. It just wouldn't be fair."

Trevor had a frustrated look on his face. "You're making a big mistake. Just give it a chance. I'm not saying that she's the one, but you need to relax and open up your heart and give the woman a chance."

The grandkids were running around the backyard with sparklers in their hands, chasing one another.

"And what if we had children? Oh, watch out, Daddy sometimes goes nuts and acts weird. He thinks he's a soldier again. What if I hit one of them or did something that would put them in danger?"

All his life, he'd wanted a son, a couple of boys to teach how to shoot, hunt, and fish and do all the manly things his own father had taught him. And he'd wanted a couple of girls to be protective of, who looked like their mother.

His family life had been good and he wanted to let his children grow up where he'd been raised. To watch them go to the rodeo, attend school, and become good men and women.

And then he'd joined the Navy. It wasn't until the jungles of Africa where he'd been on a secret mission that he'd lost his best friend. It wasn't until then that he'd seen the worst fighting of his life and thought he was going to die alongside him. Today, he knew he could never fight again because one loud boom would have him back in that forest fighting to survive.

One loud boom and his children would run fleeing from him.

"Thank you, Ms. Nash," Stacy said as she hurried back to him.

"Elizabeth," she said. "And remember what I told you."

"What did she say?"

"That is between us," Stacy said with a smile. "You're so fortunate to have a mother and family like you have, Luis."

A chuckle came from Trevor. "Your mother is working her magic. She convinced your brother he needed to marry Kalie."

"She knows better," Luis said, wishing that Stacy would tell him what they spoke about.

Stacy walked away and he hurried to catch up to her.

"Why are you walking ahead of us," he said.

"Because I didn't want to hear you talking about your mother," she replied. "She's very nice, and no, we didn't talk about you. She was asking about me. Questions every mother has a right to know about the girl their son is dating. Though we're not dating, are we?"

He swallowed hard. Why had he thought it would be a good idea to bring Stacy here tonight? "No, we're not dating; we're fucking."

A frown crossed her face and she hurried away.

"That wasn't a nice thing to say to her," Trevor said as he hurried away to go after Stacy.

What was wrong with him? Was he trying to push her away? Because seeing her with his mother had him thinking all kinds of things that he used to want. Stacy would have been the perfect wife and mother, but now he had this damn disorder that was such a hindrance.

It left him weak, and if there was anything a Navy SEAL did not want to be likened to, it was being weak.

With a sigh, he hurried after Stacy. They only had two more days and he didn't want her to be upset with him. He had been acting like an idiot.

Because if he could he, would marry her in a heartbeat. But no one deserved a wounded man and he was so impaired.

And he didn't want to be a helpless, damaged man in need of a nurse. Stacy deserved better.

CHAPTER 9

$\mathcal{S}$tacy was tempted to pack her bags and leave tonight after Luis had said such a degrading remark regarding what they had been doing all week. Sure, it was what she had agreed to; it was the truth. But the way he said it in such a debasing manner, hurt.

And the reason it hurt was because she was falling in love with him and Trevor. After speaking to his mother this evening at the party, she knew his family was exactly what she'd been dreaming of.

They were loving, caring, and concerned about one another. His mother had asked her not to hurt her son. His mom asked if she knew he had PTSD and if she could learn to live with his disorder. She'd asked Stacy if she would do everything to protect him and Trevor.

And she'd answered like she was going to be there forever, when in reality, she only had two more days with them. Two more days before she had to leave and fly home.

Stacy's own mother had never been that protective, and she admired Elizabeth Nash for trying to take care of her big strong Navy SEAL son. But his parent also asked her about Trevor and if she could accept that he was Hispanic and that his family had problems.

Everyone had problems. Her own family had suffered before she even knew the meaning of the word. Even today, what her father had done haunted her.

Trevor was one of the kindest men she'd ever met, and she didn't care about the color of his skin. All she cared about was the integrity of her men. And how they would love and care for her.

But then again, she'd agreed from the beginning that there would be no strings. No commitments. And now that agreement bothered her because she wasn't certain she could go through it without her heart breaking.

At the time, she'd never thought in a hundred years that her heart would get involved, but she loved these two men and the way they had cared for her and shown her their lifestyle and how they treated women.

No man she'd ever dated for weeks, or even months, had shown her this kind of gentle, commanding way of being cared for.

After Luis apologized to her, they had stayed at his mother's party for another thirty minutes before he wanted to leave. And maybe it was for the best because her heart was no longer in a partying kind of mood.

For the first time, she doubted her decision and wondered if she should just leave.

Naked, she swam the length of the pool, trying to soothe her hurt pride and wounded heart.

"I'm sorry," Luis said from the darkness. "Tonight, I realized that seeing you with my mother brought up so many fears. And I did everything I could to put distance between us."

Turning in the pool, she gazed at him.

"Why?"

He sighed. "Before I went into the Navy, there was a girl in college I wanted to marry and have children with. A girl I brought home to meet my family."

Licking his lips, she watched him.

"She broke my heart when she ended our engagement. I went into the Navy. John was beside me every step of the way and we were considered two of the best until he was killed. It was my fault he died. I should have protected him better."

Stacy didn't say anything but listened.

"So now I protect my heart. Whenever I fear someone is getting too close, I do everything I can to keep them away. Tonight, I realized I had done that with you."

She leaned against the wall of the pool. The lights were on, but they were dim.

"Do you think John would want you to block everyone out of your life and become a martyr for him?"

He ran his hand through his hair. "No, but no woman should have to live with me having episodes where I think I'm back in battle. What if I hurt her? What if I tried to kill her? And I can't be a father and let my children see me this way."

While she understood why he felt as he did, she just couldn't accept that was a good idea. "Too bad. It might teach your children about humility and about what can happen when you serve your country. It might make them understand that veterans should always be respected and honored and that they could be hurting."

She swam to the steps and climbed out of the pool.

"If you want me to leave, I can. I don't want you to risk me getting too close to you," she said.

He grabbed her arm. "No. Please don't go. I'm sorry. I want you to stay."

Stacy didn't know what was best. Already her heart was softening toward him and she knew she was falling in love with the two men.

Luis lifted her over his shoulder and carried her up the stairs. Trevor followed behind.

Luis dropped her on the bed.

"Spread your legs," Trevor commanded.

She licked her lips, her nerves once again roaring alive.

"Beautiful," Luis said as he stroked his cock.

Fingers pinched her nipples, sending a rushing sensation through her as she stared into Luis's emerald gaze. Heat warmed her and she swallowed hard, uncertain of the feelings they aroused within her.

Oh, how she wanted this, but her heart was on the line, and she feared she would be the one leaving broken.

Luis scooted down the bed until his mouth was even with her pussy. "I owe you this after today."

With pleasure, she watched as his tongue reached out and stroked the folds between her legs. An intense tingling sensation traveled up her spine.

She gasped. "Luis."

"Lie back and enjoy, darling. Tonight is all about you."

Every day had been about her desires, but somehow she felt like they needed to face his demons and slay them. Get them out in the open. But he would refuse her request.

Maybe this was his way of making up to her after the way he had hurt her tonight.

Spreading her open, his tongue dove inside her, and the most delicious sensations had her grasping the sheets in her fists. Heat flooded her and a moan slipped from her lips.

"Your pussy tastes sweeter than honey," he said as he licked her faster, his tongue pushing up inside, creating a spasm that had her moaning.

If this was his way of making up, she liked what he was doing.

Trevor's mouth attached to her bare breasts as his tongue encircled her nipples and he sucked on them.

One man was at her breasts and another between her legs, doing the most sensational things to her, causing her to tense and try to escape the delicious desire filling her.

She stared into Trevor's dark brown eyes as his tongue laved her breasts.

Staring at them, she became lost in the sensations these two men were creating and she felt a burgeoning sense of desire filling her, pushing her closer and closer to the edge.

Blood heated and pounded as it rushed through her, causing her lungs to squeeze as she gasped for breath.

Luis nipped at her clit and she moaned.

"Do you like that, Stacy?"

Even though there was still tension between them, part of her didn't want to admit that he was making her want him.

Luis was a good man and she feared she was going to lose him. No matter how much she wanted to give him her love, he would not let her near him. The Navy SEAL had a wall around his heart and there was no way for her to scale the barrier and reach the man she loved.

He slapped her on the butt. "Answer me."

"Yes," she said, that simple slap sending fire spiraling up to her womanly bits.

All the heat, the fire, and the inferno were building and she clenched her fists, the urge to lift her hips overwhelming her.

Suddenly she felt the buzzing in her back end and she knew they had turned on the vibrating plug. Desire seized her and she gasped.

Tonight had shown them that their time was coming to a close. Tonight felt like they were trying to hang on to the desire and the sweetness that had flowed so easily between them this week and she didn't want that time to end.

Trevor's mouth covered her own in a demanding way. This was not a gentle kiss. Oh no, his lips insisted that she surrender. His tongue invaded her mouth and commanded that she give in to the way his lips overpowered her own.

And she had demands of her own. She needed both of them tonight to prove to herself that she could walk away and not leave with a broken heart. But she wasn't certain that was possible.

His hands wrapped around her jaw and held her mouth against his own as he took what he wanted from her. And she wanted him to have everything. If only they would love her, she would give them her all. Her everything. But she didn't think that was possible for Luis. Maybe Trevor, but she even had doubts about him.

Desire had a stranglehold on her, and the pleasure building inside her was ready to explode. Why with these two did she feel such intensity all centered in her pussy and her lips?

Staring into Trevor's eyes, she melted beneath his gaze.

There was this flame, this heat between them that so far had not been extinguished.

Leaning back, he released her lips and smiled at her. "You're so beautiful when you come."

His fingers slid inside her and she gasped.

Trevor reached down between her legs and touched the little button that was nothing but nerves. His fingers rubbed over her folds while Luis's fingers slipped inside, twisting and preparing her for his cock.

A fiery heat spiraled through her and she welcomed the burn. She wanted this with her men for as long as she could hang onto the feelings they evoked.

With the vibrator creating a tsunami of desire inside her, she wouldn't last much longer.

Pleasure rippled through her and she gasped. "Luis."

"Honey, you're dripping wet," he said. "You're ready for me to fuck you."

Trevor's tongue pushed its way inside her mouth again while his fingers continued to stroke her clit. Never had she felt so many emotions at once.

So much heat. With one man, sex would be boring after this week. How mundane when she could have these two men, and yet she couldn't have them forever. And that disappointed her.

Releasing her mouth, Trevor whispered against her ear, his fingers sliding down her crack, touching her in the most private area. "We can't wait to take you here."

"Oh," she cried as his fingers circled her anus, the butt plug still safely nestled with the vibrations slower now. When he pulled it out, she felt empty, bereft until Trevor eased his finger into her back entrance, insistent and sure.

The feel of that finger probing her, swirling and demanding entry, had her moaning, raising her hips to escape the desire that ravaged her.

"Honey, I can't wait to fuck you in your ass," Trevor said, whispering into her ear.

"Do you like it?" Luis asked.

It seemed perverse, yet everything they had done to her so far, she wanted more of. She needed more.

"Yes," she whispered.

Trevor lay back and pulled Stacy on top of him, her back to his chest. His tongue reached out and licked her ear and she moaned. "I'm not going to take your ass tonight, but soon. And darling, I can't wait for the two of us to take you together. Claiming you at the same time, filling all your holes is what we want more than anything."

His words sent a shiver through her. The sound of his voice and his steely resolve left her heated. There was no doubt that eventually, they would both take her at the same time. And part of her anticipated and dreaded that double invasion.

Tonight, she was not going to think about when that would happen and how it would feel. Tonight, she needed to experience them making her feel wanted. Making her forget that Luis had made what they had together feel cheap.

Luis removed his fingers from inside her and crawled on the bed to her. She was sandwiched in between the two men and she moaned at the feel of their naked flesh against her own, the strength in their bodies and their hardness against her softness.

His long, hard dick jutted out in front of him like a sword. The feeling of being sandwiched between them was like nothing she'd ever experienced. It was like they enfolded her into their bodies.

She felt protected, she felt cherished, and soon she would return to New York.

Luis placed his sheathed rigid penis at the entrance to her pussy. What was he waiting for? She wanted him.

"Do you want me to fuck you?"

Was this because of what he'd said earlier tonight? Was it wrong to want him to take her?

"You know I do," she said. "I want both of you to take me together. As one."

She gazed into his eyes and he reached out and stroked her face.

"I want to hear you scream my name," he said.

"Only if you do it right," she whispered.

A grin spread across his face. "You know I will."

She shrugged. "I know nothing after tonight."

The words were enough to cause her breathing to increase and her heart to hammer in her chest. Tonight, she wanted to make him work hard to get her to come.

A frown appeared between Luis's eyes and he focused on her before he reached down, parted the folds between her legs, and rubbed the little nub there. Pleasure spiked through her and she moaned and lifted her hips as if to urge him to fuck her.

"How does that feel?" he asked.

"Better, but you're not there yet," she said.

With his hand, he slapped her on the pussy, sending tremors rippling through her.

"How about now?"

"You're getting closer," she said, gazing at him, wanting to punish him for what he'd said.

He slapped her again, but this time his fingers lingered on her clit and he shoved two inside her pressing her G-spot.

"Oh," she cried, her hips rising to the passion he was creating.

"And now?"

"Luis, if you don't fuck me, I'm going to jump on Trevor," she said.

A grin spread across his face. "About time."

Luis moved forward and entered her pussy while his fingers continued to rub that little pleasure nub that almost had her begging him to take her.

She groaned as her body accommodated him, stretching to accept his long cock as he filled her.

Both of them had nice sized cocks that gave her pleasure.

"And now, I'm going to make you scream when you come this time."

Slowly he moved inside her, the friction creating heat and her breathing became difficult. It was the most incredible feeling, and while he went slowly, she suddenly wanted him to hurry.

"Luis," she said. "I need—"

"What, darling? Tell me," he said as he continued to fuck her while Trevor held her, twisting her nipples with his fingers.

"I need you," she said.

Suddenly he stopped.

Gazing at him, she wondered what he was doing.

"Beg me to fuck you," he said.

There was still tension between them. A need to push one another as far as they could without either getting angry.

"Only if you'll put the butt plug back in," she said.

He grinned at her. "I'm calling the shots here, darling, not you. Now beg or you're not coming."

With a growl, she glared at him. "Luis, please I need you to fuck me."

A smirk spread across his face and he continued ramming his cock inside her pussy. And then he picked up the butt plug and handed it to Trevor, who promptly shoved it in her ass.

Then he turned on the vibration and her body began to shimmy.

There was no room. She was filled to capacity with his cock and the butt plug and she knew this would be how it would feel when they both took her.

"I'm going to come," she cried.

"Not without me," he said and slapped her on the ass, Trevor maneuvering the butt plug, sliding it in and out.

"Come now," he cried.

Trevor whispered against her ear, his breath warm and tingly. "That's it, sweetheart, open up for me. Take me inside your ass. Let me fill you while Luis fills your pussy. Let us both give you pleasure."

And they were. Never before had she felt such heat and fire building. She squealed at the pain and pleasure that exploded inside her with Luis's cock and the butt plug. She felt them going back and forth inside her body, the heat growing. The fire raged and she felt her orgasm roar toward her.

"Luis," she screamed as she clenched his cock inside her tightly. Waves of desire filled her, and for a moment, she felt like she would drown as she gulped for air.

He exploded inside her, and for the first time, she was grateful he was using a condom. No unwanted pregnancies.

Trevor held her body as she shook and jerked, the passion cresting, returning her to earth, spent.

Luis collapsed beside her. "You need to take care of Trevor."

With a smile, she turned toward Trevor.

"Up on your knees. I want to take you from behind. I want to spank that delicious full ass of yours. I want to shove my cock in your sweet pussy so deep while my fingers stroke your ass. So, yes, you better be ready."

His words were rough, and yet they left her longing, wanting more. Yearning spiraled through Stacy and slowly she rose to her knees.

Trevor moved behind her with Luis now beneath her. Trevor rubbed his hand over her buttocks, creating a delicious warmth. "Sorry, darling, but I want to hear you moan."

Slap! He hit her buttocks with his hand.

Shock and a stinging sensation rippled through her all the way to her pussy. Heat seared her ass and yet it was a delicious warmth that left her wanting more. "Trevor."

"One more time," he said as his hand connected with her ass. It burned but the heat created a fire inside. A fire that centered in her middle.

With a sigh, he pushed her forward until her head rested on Luis's chest, her ass in the air.

"Now that's the sight I've been waiting to see. Your cheeks slightly pink from my hand, your pussy dripping with want for me, and your ass just begging to be fucked."

Moaning, she glanced back at him and blew him a kiss. It seemed to spur him on as he plunged into her waiting pussy.

A groan escaped her, not from pain, but pleasure as Luis's lips consumed hers, Trevor hammering into her pussy. This was no gentle fucking, but rough sex.

And strangely she loved it. The power of her two men being in control, giving her pleasure was something she'd never experienced.

How could she leave them and return to her boring life in New York? How?

As Luis's kiss commanded her surrender, his lips ravaged hers, his tongue demanding entry, his fingers twisting her nipples. Oh, how she loved the way that Luis kissed and the way Trevor slammed his cock into her again and again.

Needing to draw as much air into her lungs as possible, Stacy felt another orgasm building within her.

The bed squeaked, the mattress hitting the back wall as Trevor pounded into her over and over.

"Don't come," he commanded. The need was building, roaring through her, and at any moment, she would tumble over the edge.

"I can't…"

Smack! He hit her ass with his palm and lifted her hips to meet him. A scream formed inside of her that would soon be released.

"Do it again."

Smack, he hit her ass again, sending vibrations through the butt plug. The orgasm rushed at her and there would be no holding back.

"Now. Now, you can come," he cried as his body shook as he came.

A scream tore from her throat. "Trevor. Oh, Trevor."

Luis held her in his arms while she writhed and convulsed. Finally, they collapsed onto the bed totally spent.

Exhausted, Trevor and Luis arranged Stacy until she lay between them.

"Am I forgiven?" Luis asked, his breathing rapid.

Yes, he'd been forgiven, but with her falling for him, she didn't want to give in to him so easily.

"You're well on the way, but I think you may have to try again," she said with a giggle.

Luis rose from the bed and went into the bathroom. When he returned his face was white.

They both gazed at him. Stacy felt concerned that he might be having another episode. "What's wrong?"

"The condom broke. I came inside your pussy."

It was the first time she'd seen real fear on his face except for when he was having the episode. Did he fear her getting pregnant or something even worse?

What could she say?

CHAPTER 10

Two more days. That's all that was left before Stacy had to leave to return to New York. Two days and Luis wasn't ready for this to end. And yet, he couldn't promise her anything. He couldn't even tell her that next week things would be different. It wouldn't be fair to her if he asked her to stay.

Sitting in the kitchen sipping on his first cup of coffee, he glanced outside and saw Trevor coming back from the barn. It was early. The sun had just risen and he had left their bed, unable to sleep.

Fear had ridden him hard all night long. Fear that somehow he had impregnated Stacy with the broken condom. And yet he was the only one who seemed to be concerned. But he couldn't be a father.

The sun was up, but that was about all.

Trevor walked in the door with a basket of fresh eggs.

"The chickens were productive yesterday. We have almost a dozen fresh eggs," he said taking them to the sink and rinsing them off.

Luis wished he would do that outside, but he'd clean the sink after Trevor left the kitchen. Chicken poop was not something he wanted in the house sink.

A pregnancy was something he didn't want either, not with him suffering episodes of PTSD.

"Are you all right?" Trevor asked. "Yesterday, you really concerned me."

Last night was what concerned him. He'd learned to live with coming out of an episode to people staring at him like he'd lost his mind.

"I'm fine as long as no loud noise startles me," he said.

Last night, he had a hard time sleeping. The image of his mother and the excited way she had spoken to Stacy played in his head. When he told her that Stacy returned to New York, he was going to break his mother's heart.

They were not getting married as much as he liked the idea. No woman deserved to have to live with a man who often returned to battle.

He was the only one who seemed concerned about his PTSD episodes, the others seemed to accept it as a part of him.

But he wasn't ready to accept that. All night, he'd lay there thinking about the condom breaking with Stacy. What if she were pregnant?

As much as he enjoyed her, he was not ready to settle down, and he never wanted children to witness their father going crazy. It just couldn't happen.

This morning the answer to his problems had come to him out of the blue. And while it wasn't the perfect solution, he knew it would keep him from worrying about an unwanted pregnancy.

"If I make an appointment to get a vasectomy, would you take me to the doctor?"

Trevor turned from the sink and stared at him. "Are you certain about this? You always wanted children before you went into the Navy."

If his mother ever learned the truth, she would be so upset with him. But after the scare last night, it was better that he take care of it. That way a breaking condom wouldn't put the fear of God into him.

"Little children would be terrified if they saw me having an episode. They would be so afraid of Daddy and it wouldn't be fair to them."

Trevor seemed frustrated and Luis didn't understand why. Before, they had always understood one another.

"What about if you were married? Would you tell the woman before you married her that you will never have children with her? We had planned on marrying a woman and sharing her. I want children. I want a wife and family. I want it all. And now after we've bought the ranch, you're changing your mind. That's not fair to me."

This was the hard part. This was the part that Luis wasn't certain about. And yet it wouldn't be right for anyone's children to see him fighting an unseen battle.

"We had always planned on it being the two of us sharing a woman."

"Someone like Stacy," Trevor said. "Have you considered that most women want children? If they find out you got a vasectomy the woman is not going to be happy."

That thought had swirled around in his head, and he knew if he married, eventually something would happen and he'd have babies. A family. And yet his chest warmed with the idea of a little boy who looked like him or a little girl who looked like…Stacy.

"It would be for the best if I never had children," he said. "I don't want them to be afraid of me or to think I'm some kind of monster."

Trevor sighed. "Give it time, man. You don't want to do something rash that you can't undo."

Last night when he'd gone in the bathroom and seen the ripped condom, he'd known that he was taking a huge risk on Stacy or any woman getting pregnant.

Stacy walked into the kitchen, looking very sleepy and sexy, and oh, how he wanted to lay her out on the table and give her a proper good morning.

"Good morning," she said with a yawn.

"Good morning," Trevor said.

Right now, Luis couldn't say anything as he stared at her naked. What if she was expecting his child even now? No. Just no. That couldn't happen.

Luis pulled her down onto his lap and let his hands run down her spine to her buttocks.

"Did you sleep well?"

"Yes," she said. "Just not long enough. Someone kept fucking me last night."

"Who was he? I'll kill him," he said.

She giggled. "You."

"Oh," he said.

"The one who tore through a condom," she replied, laughing at the idea.

A niggle of worry scurried up his spine. "Won't happen again."

She gazed at him. "Why not? I'm not worried about it. Why would you be?"

"I'm thinking of getting a vasectomy," he said. "The condom might tear again, but at least I won't have to worry about getting you pregnant."

Her body tensed in his arms and she stood. Her face had an odd look on it as she turned and glared at him.

"Why would you do that? Don't you want a family? Children? What about your wife? Shouldn't she have a say in this decision?"

Turning her back to him, she walked to the coffee pot and poured herself a cup. From the expression on her face, he could see she was angry. Why would it matter to her?

This was his decision.

"If I had a family, how would they handle it when I had an episode? You saw how I acted. I thought I was in combat. I was fighting the enemy. What if I grabbed a gun and tried to shoot one of the kids, believing they were the people I was after? No child needs to be around a man who suffers like I do."

For a moment, nothing was said and then she sank down at the table. Her hands were shaking. There was an uneasiness in the kitchen that he was shocked to feel. This was his decision and no one else's. She had no right to get mad at him. There were no commitments between them.

"All my life, I wanted brothers and sisters," she said, taking a sip of coffee. "My mother had a very hard time delivering me. She was in labor for over twenty-four hours. My father was right there at her side, but he swore she would never suffer like that again. So the day after they had me, he got a vasectomy. He didn't consult my mother. He didn't talk to her doctor. He just went and did it."

She sat the coffee cup down on the table. "What he didn't know was that first babies are often the hardest to deliver, the next one could have been easier. Because of him, I have no brothers or sisters. My mother was so upset when she kept trying to get pregnant and then he finally told her the truth. A year later he died in the Twin Towers attack. It was just the two of us from then on."

Stunned, Luis sat there and knew that Stacy would never forgive him.

"But I have PTSD. Children should never be around me," he said.

"And it may go away," Stacy said. "We're not married. But I would tell you right now, that would be a deal breaker for me. I want a family. Children, babies. I know there will always be problems you have to deal with, but for you to just give up and get a vasectomy seems like a coward's way out."

"I'm not a coward," he said getting angry.

"The hell you aren't," she said, standing and leaving the kitchen.

Stunned, he sat there staring at his coffee. He was tempted to follow her and finish this conversation, but then he decided that no, it would be best to let them both calm down. Besides, why was she so upset?

They had agreed that this week would be just for fun, and yet she acted like his decision would ruin everything. She was leaving the day after tomorrow. He doubted they would ever see each other again.

"Why does this feel like it's going to ruin our remaining

time?" Trevor said. "You must know this changes everything between you and me as well."

"I know," Luis said standing. "I'm going to see my family."

Trevor nodded. "I'll call my mother and check on her. See what my little brother has done now. I'll be out in the lab if you need me. And leave Stacy alone. I think she needs some time to think about why she cares what you do. We agreed to no promises. But I think we're all finding that really hard right now. At least, I am."

It was true, they had all said this would be a week of pleasure and sex, and now he worried about her opinion. He wanted more than just this week. But if she wanted a family, she would drop him like a hot rock.

An hour later, he sat in front of his mother at the kitchen table, a cup of coffee in front of him.

"It's kind of odd to see you here during the week. Is everything all right?"

"Everything's fine," he said knowing it wasn't.

"Your father and I really like Stacy. And you and Trevor would make the perfect husbands for that girl."

He nodded and sighed. But Stacy would not want him if he got a vasectomy.

"Mom, you know I have PTSD," he said.

"Yes," she replied. "But you're seeing that military doctor, aren't you?"

"Yes," he said but it had been over two months since he'd seen him. It was never a pleasant experience to sit there and relive the events that bothered him. Especially, the one where John died. All it did was upset him.

"What's going on, Luis," she said gazing at him. "Is it Stacy?"

That was the problem. It was Stacy and yet it wasn't her fault.

"She's leaving on Saturday," he said. "I don't know if we'll ever see her again."

She nodded. "Do you want to see her again?"

Did he? Of course, he did. Maybe that was what was bugging him. She was leaving and he didn't want her to go. And yet he kept trying to push her away because he didn't want to get too close to her.

"You know, son, since you've come home from the service, you never let people get close to you. It must be terribly frustrating to a woman. Especially one who doesn't understand our ways. Your job is to show her how the men in our community look after and care for the women here."

As far as he was concerned, he'd done all that. He'd been protective of her, at least he thought he had. When they were having sex, everything between them was fine. But the last two days, he'd noticed that it felt like something more, and that scared him.

"If I let people get close to me, they'll see the scars left from the war. Yesterday, I had an episode before we came to your party."

"And how did Stacy handle it," she asked.

That was the problem. She'd handled it very well. So well, that he could see himself confiding in her. He could see himself relaxing with her and letting his guard down. He could see her convincing him that they should have a family.

"She was excellent," he said. "She was comforting. She and Trevor brought me back from the battle where John died. But, Mom, no one should ever have to do that. No one. I can't depend on Trevor and Stacy to always be there when I go nuts."

"You do not go nuts," she said. "You just return back to the battles that affected you the most. The ones that hurt so badly when you lost someone you cared about. And if you don't trust Trevor and Stacy, you could lose them as well."

She was right. He could already see that Trevor was questioning everything since he didn't want to marry and settle down with a wife and create a family. And Stacy...she wouldn't accept him if he didn't want children. She just wouldn't.

"Mom, I did something really stupid this morning," he said. "Really stupid."

A frown spread across her face. "What? I'm sure it can be corrected."

"I'm not so certain. Last night, the condom broke and I was scared that I had impregnated Stacy."

His mother giggled. "I couldn't be happier."

"No," he said. "It wouldn't be right to tie her down to a man who has episodes and relives battles. And our children? What if I hurt one of them or frightened them?"

Reaching out she took his hand. "Luis, if Stacy is the right woman for you, if she loves you, none of that will matter. She'll do her best to protect you. She'll make certain that your children understand. Honestly, I think if she loves you, she'll cure you of the past. I have nothing to prove that. But I truly believe that love heals a person. And you, dear son, deserve to be healed."

Astonished, he stared at his mother. Was she right? Would love heal him of these nightmares?

"Think of it this way. What if you didn't take a chance with

Stacy? What if you let her go back to New York and never saw her again? Will you always wonder if she was the one who could have made you whole?"

With a sigh, he shook his head. "You didn't let me get to the part where I was stupid."

Her brows rose. "What did you do?"

"I told her I was going to get a vasectomy so that I could never get a woman pregnant," he said.

Shaking her head, his mother sighed. "That was stupid. And how did she react?"

"She got mad," he said. "But I only wanted to protect her and any children we ever had from them seeing me act like a crazy man."

"You are not crazy, but I'm on her side. I'd have been mad as well. Most women want children and grandchildren. They want a family line. Their husband's child. What did she say?"

"She wants a big family," he said, not wanting to tell his mother what her father had done. That was not his place.

"Are you going to do it?"

"I don't know what to do. I don't want to lose Stacy and this would end it between us. I know for certain, she would not accept me if I had a vasectomy."

"And how did Trevor feel?"

He didn't know how to react to Trevor. They had been friends for so long and had planned on sharing a woman between them.

"He was frustrated. He said he wanted us to share a wife and family and my plan would not work for him or our wife."

She gave him the motherly look that said you're *doing this all wrong.*

"But, Mom, I'm damaged goods."

"No, son, you're not. You wanted kids at one time."

"Yes," he said.

"If you didn't have this problem, would you still want children?"

He thought for a moment. "Yes."

His mother leaned back. "That tells me that if you were cured or healed or had fewer episodes, you'd want a family. What if you did the vasectomy and then you were cured? Think of what you would have missed out on."

He sat there silent for a moment thinking of a little boy who looked like him and a girl who looked like Stacy. If he was cured, he would want that and Trevor's children as well.

"This is your decision, son, but I think you know the answer. And I think you better get back over to your house before Stacy gives up on you. If I were her, I'd already have my bags packed and I'd be leaving. Not having children would be a deal breaker for me and I'd go home."

Terror struck his chest. No, she wasn't leaving until Saturday. They had tomorrow still. They had time to talk about this and maybe even work things out. And he wanted to make things work with Stacy.

Hell, he didn't want her to leave.

An urgency filled him. Standing, he leaned down and hugged his mother.

"Thanks, Mom," he said. "I better get back to the ranch."

"Remember, son, love heals and you deserve just as much happiness as you can stand. Tell Stacy we said hello."

Walking out to his truck, he tried to call Trevor. The man didn't answer.

CHAPTER 11

Standing in the shower, she let the tears run down her face. The condom tear was ripping them apart and exposing the weakness in her dreams of being in a relationship with them. It had been her dream to have children. A family of her own and with Luis's announcement this morning, the ugliness of her past had reared its head.

Her father's actions had hurt more than just her mother. He'd also kept her from having siblings to share her life with, to grow up with.

Why was it that when she found the two men she was falling in love with there was another problem?

Oh, she'd come close a couple of times to falling in love with other men, but they always had some terrible flaw.

Well, this morning, she'd found the flaw in this relationship. And it hurt so much, she didn't think she could continue.

But these two were so special, and when she learned that Luis was getting a vasectomy, the past slammed into her. Why her mother never married after her father's death, she didn't understand. She and her mother were alone in this world and when others were gathering for the holidays, they stayed home.

She had found two men she loved, but they didn't want the same things in life that she insisted on. And after being a lonely, only child, she wanted a family with lots of little ones running from room to room.

Maybe it was time to load up the car and leave. Maybe it was time to return to New York and nurse her broken heart.

It had been so wonderful, so much fun, and she enjoyed every minute of how they'd made love to her. They had planned on a week with no commitments, but sometime during this time, she'd begun to care. Sometime during the week, her heart became committed and yet they were still only thinking six days.

Now gazing at them, she knew they were who she wanted, and yet she still couldn't have them.

She loved Luis for being such a big strong man who made certain she was well taken care of. The way he was serious and yet comforting and gentle. And she loved Trevor for being the family man who wanted the best for his brothers and sisters, and how he made her laugh and was such a smart man who made her think in ways she'd never considered.

They were the perfect combination except Luis didn't want children.

Having a family had been her dream for years. And no, she couldn't give it up.

She wanted to birth a child, watch them grow up and help them make the right choices in life. If she had to do it alone, she would. And if she were pregnant, she would never tell Luis. It would be her secret.

Stepping out of the shower, she dried her tears. It was time to leave. This week had been fun, but now she couldn't look at them with her heart involved and knowing they didn't want the same things she wanted in life.

Heartbreak was inevitable and it was better to leave now before they saw her pain.

She removed the final butt plug, realizing they would never fulfill her dream of them both taking her at the same time. That was something she'd just have to fantasize about.

Time to go home. Back to New York City and the job she abhorred. Back to the life of working nine to five. Back to looking for a man who would fulfill her desires and also give her the life she dreamed of.

Quickly she dressed and packed her suitcase.

The house was quiet. When she glanced out the window, she saw that Luis's truck was gone. Maybe he'd already gotten his appointment and was scheduled to receive his snip and tuck. But she didn't want to know.

Where was Trevor?

After she had packed everything, she wrote a note to them so they wouldn't come searching for her. It was past time to leave. It was time to sever all communication and go back to her real life.

As she wrote the note, her tears flowed, and she knew this was going to be a long, sad trip. She'd thought there might be a chance for the three of them to settle down and create the family she longed for.

But that was just a dream. A dream she had to get over. A dream she should never have considered.

Laying the note on the desk, she picked up her suitcase and purse and headed down the stairs, hoping that she would not run into either of them. It would be better to leave without having to face them because she knew she would cry.

When she reached her car, she stopped and gazed out at the ranch. It was such a beautiful piece of property. A little piece of Texas that she'd grown to love. But it wasn't meant for her.

Her happiness did not exist here and it was time to go back to the city.

Climbing into the car, she pushed the button to start the engine and then she backed out, hoping she wasn't making the biggest mistake of her life leaving a piece of her heart right here at the ranch with these two wonderful cowboys. Two wonderful men, who couldn't give her what she wanted. A family.

How could she have given them her heart in less than a week? Because they were exactly the kind of men she'd been looking for. Only one major problem kept her from staying.

Pulling out of the gate, she didn't look back. It was time to look forward and keep her eyes on the road, though she felt like the car was dragging her heart along the road.

When she reached San Antonio, she returned the rental car and caught the red-eye to New York. Looking down at her phone, she turned it off, hoping they didn't have her cell phone number.

She needed a chance to heal. A chance to get over the feelings that had her heart breaking. As the flight took off, a tear slipped down her cheek as they flew over the early morning lights of the city of San Antonio.

She was leaving a piece of her heart behind and she turned her face to the window, knowing that her next stop would be back to her old life.

Time to put this week behind her. Time to forget about the two handsome cowboys who had given her a taste of paradise.

Luis drove like a crazy man from his parents' house to the ranch, breaking speed limits and taking chances. Hurrying to get back and praying that his mother was wrong.

When Luis pulled his truck up into the drive, he saw her rental car was gone. They hadn't moved it since that first night. His chest tightened at the sight of the empty drive.

Slamming his fist against the steering wheel, he screamed. What had he done?

Why in the hell could his mother be so right and know what Stacy was feeling? She was a woman that's why. A brilliant woman who knew how to read people. Who understood a woman's need. And he'd fucked up today in the worst possible way.

Jumping out of the truck, he ran into the house, slamming the door behind him.

"Stacy," he yelled, hoping she was still here, knowing instinctively that she was gone. Silence filled the house except for his labored breathing and the sound of his boots on the wood floors.

"Stacy," he screamed again.

Running up the stairs, he entered the bedroom and saw that her suitcase was gone. The last butt plug lay on the desk along with a note.

A searing pain, the agony of loss, struck him in the chest. The last time he'd experienced this was when John was killed. His hands shook as he picked up the letter from Stacy.

Dear Luis and Trevor,

Thank you for such a wonderful week. I wish we could have completed the final act, but I need to go home. Though we made a promise there would be no commitments this week, after five days, my heart was getting involved. And I can't give up my dreams even for you, Luis.

You two were the best men I've ever had the pleasure of being with, and to keep my promise, I knew I had to return home. Having a family is a dream I've had for years and I'll never give it up. When Luis mentioned he would never marry or have children, I knew that would crush me and so I made the decision to leave before I fell in love with the two of you even more.

Yes, I was falling in love with both of you, even though it's been less than a week.

Again, thank you for the best week of my life. I'll always have a special place for the two of you in my heart. Please don't call me or come after me. I need this time to heal. Luis doesn't want to marry or have a family and I want that more than anything.

I wish you both the very best.

Stacy

Stunned, Luis read the note and sighed. He'd fucked things up royally and yet he still had misgivings. What if love didn't heal him? What if he remained this way for the rest of his life?

What if his nightmares grew worse?

Stacy had been wonderful when he had the one episode, but to deal with that on a regular basis, she would soon grow weary and think him broken. And he never wanted to be considered beyond help.

The bedroom door opened and Trevor walked in.

"Her car's gone," he said. "Did she leave?"

Luis handed him the note, his heart heavy.

With a sigh, Trevor sank down on the bed and Luis could see he was angry.

Shaking his head, he got up, went to the closet, and pulled out a suitcase.

"Something's come up and I've got to get to Houston," he said.

Trevor was angry that Stacy had left. Luis had screwed everything up. Even his best friend was mad at him. And he couldn't blame him.

"I'm sorry, Trevor," he said. "I'm confused. I don't know what to do. You know how bad my episodes can be. You've seen them. A child would be terrified."

His friend turned and faced him, his brown eyes flashing with anger.

"She was the best thing that has ever happened to us. And this morning, you made the announcement about getting a vasectomy all because one condom ripped. Yes, you've got PTSD, but do you honestly think it will last forever?"

"My mother told me that she thinks I'll heal. I'm not so certain, but it is a first step."

"Not if you don't go back to the doctor you were seeing,"

he said, throwing clothes into a bag. "Start by getting back in to see that doctor you're avoiding. I can't imagine what you went through when you were in the Navy, but it's time to put it behind you. I'm ready to settle down and have a family. And you have to decide if that's something you want."

Trevor was right. At first, he'd refused to face his PTSD head-on, but maybe he needed to talk to the doctor and see if he could put this part of his life behind him. Maybe he never would. Maybe he would have flareups, but regardless, it was time to learn the truth.

"I'll call him today and see when I can get in to see him," he said.

Trevor threw in his toiletries.

"What about Stacy?" Luis said. "What are we going to do?"

"Do you have her phone number?"

"No," he said, realizing they didn't have her number or her address. All they knew was that she lived in New York City. But Kalie knew how to contact her. Kalie knew where she lived.

"Maybe we need to let her have some time to think about this. Maybe we need some time to consider what we want. This was supposed to have been a week that we just engaged in pleasure and sex with no commitments, but things changed for her. And frankly, for me as well. I was thinking we'd found our forever woman until this morning when you let her know you didn't want children. Which was a shock to me as well. Did you even think about letting me know?"

It was something he had not wanted to discuss because he feared exactly what was happening now. Trevor wanted a family. Trevor wanted them to share a woman and get married. If he had to face this problem and an ultimatum, he dreaded he'd lose another friend.

"I kept hoping we would never have to cross this bridge," he said, knowing he was not being fair to his friend or to Stacy.

With a sigh, Luis knew Trevor had been considering asking her to stay. They were so good together. The sex had been fantastic and they enjoyed one another's company. Stacy had been so eager to learn their ways and willing to try just about anything.

Only his PTSD stood in the way.

Was that why he'd acted like he had this morning? Things had been so good and he had to fuck it all up? Was this his way of pushing her and even Trevor away?

"My mother told me that I push people away to keep them from getting close. I think I did that this morning. After the condom broke last night, I got scared. I was developing feelings for Stacy and I had to push her away so she didn't see the pain inside me. Even you, Trevor, I push away," he admitted.

Trevor nodded and continued to pack a suitcase. The man was leaving. Luis had ruined everything between the three of them.

Outside, the big elm tree's leaves rustled in the wind and the cows bellowed in the distance. Being here by himself, it would be quiet. Lonely.

With a sigh, Trevor ran his hand through his hair. "This week, I started thinking of forever. Of you, me, and Stacy building a life together. But after this morning, I need some time away. When I get back, we need to see if we want to continue the ranch or go our separate ways. You need to let me know what you want to do. But for me, I want a family. I want to get married and build a life either here on the ranch or someplace. That can happen either with you or without you, but that's what I want. Now you have to decide what you want."

Luis nodded. Why did it feel like not only had he screwed things up with Stacy, but that he was going to possibly lose his best friend? All because of his stupid PTSD that he feared. Was he willing to lose everything?

Hadn't he lost enough?

Closing his suitcase, Trevor gazed at him. "You know I love you, Luis. We've been friends for years, but I have dreams. Dreams of my own family. Dreams of a wife and kids. I always thought we would share this, but if you insist on no children, then that's not going to work for me. Think about what you want. I'll be back next week and we can talk then, but I'm not giving up my dreams for you."

Lifting his suitcase, he walked out the door and Luis heard him go down the stairs and out the door. A few minutes later, he heard Trevor's truck back out the driveway, gravel spinning.

Two people had walked out of his life today and it felt like his world was crashing down around him.

Sitting alone in the bedroom, he noticed how quiet the house was. Unable to function, he just sat there for the longest. Finally, he went downstairs into the living room, found a bottle of scotch, and took it outside.

Sitting out on the patio, he watched the sun set, drinking his scotch and remembering how Stacy looked swimming naked in the pool. How the time they spent together had been the best time of his life. And he'd screwed it all up.

His chest ached with the loss of her and he continued to drink until the bottle was damn near empty.

Was this what he wanted? An empty house? Silence, being alone?

In the moonlight, John's image appeared before him, shimmering in the darkness. Bleary- eyed, he stared at the best friend he'd lost in the war. The man who had taken a bullet meant for him. The man he still mourned.

"I'm dead, but you're alive. Don't fuck up the life you have. Grow up and learn to live. Time to get over my death, Luis, and live your life. Don't disappoint me, soldier."

With a shimmer, the image disappeared. Before each battle, they would turn to one another and say, "Don't disappoint me, soldier."

Sitting there he thought about his life and how he'd changed from a young man into the man he was today. Shaking his head, a tear traveled down his face. "Don't disappoint me, soldier."

Standing, Luis went into the house and put away the bottle of scotch. Then he called Dr. Richards. Time to seek help. Time not to disappoint those who had given their lives for him.

CHAPTER 13

Trevor stayed away for a week. During that time he visited with his family, went into Houston, and thought about what he really wanted in life.

As much as he loved Luis – his brother, his best friend, his partner at the ranch – he wanted more.

Why had he made all this money if he was not going to leave it behind to his children? Or help them get ahead in life, give them a better childhood than he'd experienced.

It was his reason for helping his brothers and sisters. He wanted them to have better lives. And he wanted a son or daughter to take over his business someday.

With Stacy, he'd begun to have hope that maybe they'd found the woman to give them what they were searching for. Sure, Luis kept saying he would never get married, but Trevor had hoped and prayed that was just the result of the PTSD and that once he got it under control, he would change his mind.

How could one stupid ripped condom create so much

havoc in their life? But one thing it had done was bring everything into the open. Now they would make the decisions that were necessary for them each to find the happiness they wanted in their lives.

Today would be a monumental day in his life. Today, he would decide whether or not the dreams of them owning a ranch together and creating a family were still viable. Today could be the end of the friendship they'd had for nearly twenty years. Today, they could go their own separate ways.

Pulling up in front of the ranch, he noticed that Luis's truck was there. After he parked, he stepped out of the vehicle and breathed in the clean fresh air. Home. The sound of a cow mooing in the distance filled him with happiness.

It would be so hard to let this go. And he wondered if he could buy out Luis if Luis decided that marriage and a family were not for him.

When he walked inside, the house was empty. On the back patio, he found his friend gazing out at the pool and the pastures beyond it.

"Hey, you're back," Luis said. "How was Houston?"

"The same city that I left," he said so thankful he was out of the hustle and bustle. "How are you?"

"I'm good," he said. "We need to talk. I owe you a huge apology."

That was a good way to start. But had he made any decisions regarding Stacy? About having a family? Trevor was more certain than ever that he wanted a wife and children. The path of his life had become crystal clear in the week he was gone.

"Thank you," he said. But he didn't say anything else

because he wanted Luis to bring up if he had come to his senses. But what if he hadn't? Then they would need to decide on who got the ranch or if they wanted to sell the place and each start over.

"I've seen Dr. Richards twice this week. He told me that before I wasn't interested in getting better. This time he says he can see a difference in me and wanted to know what happened. I told him about Stacy."

With a sigh, Luis got up from the patio table and shuffled toward the pool. Trevor followed him. "All I could do was sit here every night and think about how beautiful she looked naked swimming laps in our pool. How she fit in with us. How she satisfied us better than any woman I've ever experienced."

Trevor nodded. "I've missed her all week. The smell of her. The way she made me feel like a man and she was all woman."

Still Luis had not said the words Trevor needed to hear for their partnership to continue. Maybe he didn't realize it, but today was the deadline. Time for him to make a choice.

Because Trevor had decided the moment had come for him to launch his life plan. He wasn't getting any younger.

With a sigh, Luis gazed out at the pasture. "This place means a lot to me. You and I have worked so hard to get to this place in life where we can relax and enjoy our lives. Share it with another person. Dr. Richards asked me a lot of questions about my visions. About how I would feel being alone."

Trevor heard the pain in his voice. The last week had been so lonely for him and it was why he'd come to the conclusion that it was decision time. He was tired of being lonely and he wanted to share his success with someone besides his family.

"That first night after you left, I got drunk. Very drunk and either my mind played tricks on me or John came to visit me. He said don't fuck up the life I have. Make a decision and learn to live. Get over his death. 'Don't disappoint me, soldier.'"

Luis walked over to a chair. "It was right here in this spot that he came to me. I don't believe in ghosts, but something felt right. It was like he was reaching out from the grave and telling me to stop ruining my life. To live the life I've always dreamed of. To stop fucking it up."

Trevor shook his head. That was the weirdest story he'd ever heard, but if it reached Luis, then he was glad.

"As soon as I could, I called Dr. Richards. I'm going to see him again in a few days. I'm working on getting better," he said. "He's telling me that if I work hard, I may get over this."

Trevor was filled with relief. But Luis still had not said if he wanted to marry and have children.

"I miss Stacy," he said. "My heart is breaking, I miss her so much. I've tried to find her cell phone number. I even called Kalie and asked her to give me her number, but she refused. But I did find her address."

Warmth filled Trevor. Did this mean what he hoped it meant?

"I want her back," he said.

"Me too," Trevor said.

"Let's go find her," he said.

"Not yet," Trevor replied. "I'm not going to go find her for her only to walk away from us again. Are you ready to commit to her on her terms? To have a family and not get a vasectomy?"

Luis sighed and ran his hand through his hair. "I'm scared as hell, but yes, if that's what it takes to get her back, then I'll get her pregnant as soon as we see her again."

Hope filled Trevor. "I'm serious. I want to ask her to marry us. For us to bring her home to Texas and create a life together. I want her here, not working some job, but to make our ranch into a home. I want to hear the pitter-patter of little kids running up and down the stairs. I want to see our baby filling her belly. And if that's not what you want, then let me know now."

Nodding, Luis grinned. "All I want is for Stacy to be in our lives and to give her whatever will make her happy. And if that's half a dozen kids, then let's get started. Will I still have episodes? Probably, at least for a while, but I'm going to continue working with Dr. Richards. I'm not going to give up on facing my fears and overcoming them. Being with you and Stacy is more important to me than those damn demons."

Trevor could hardly contain his excitement. "I came home, worrying that our partnership was going to end, but I know you're a good man who will do whatever it takes to get over your disorder. And even if you never are fully over the episodes, Stacy and I will protect you and do our best to make certain no one sees them but us. Including our children. Now let's go get our girl. If we get to San Antonio tonight, we could catch the red-eye to New York."

A big smile filled Luis's face, and for the first time since he'd returned from the Navy, Trevor sensed a peace about him. If nothing else, Stacy's leaving had made him face that he needed to get help. And Trevor believed she would stay on him to continue.

There was hope and that filled his chest with such happiness.

"Let's go," Luis said. He reached out and hugged his friend. "Thank you for sticking by me. I was afraid I'd lost both of you."

"You came mighty close," Trevor said. "Now come on, let's go get our girl."

CHAPTER 14

Ten days away from where she'd grown up, and when Stacy returned, she realized she hated living in the Big Apple. Sure it had its advantages. She didn't need a car; she could travel by bus or subway or even taxi to anywhere she wanted. But it was the hustle and bustle of the city that really got to her.

She missed hearing the birds early in the morning, the cows mooing, the buzz of the hummingbirds, and the snort of a horse as it stood in the pasture. She would've thought she would have missed the honking taxis, the constant movement of people as they hurried down the street, the street performers, everything she was accustomed to, but it was like something had awakened inside her. Something that loved the peacefulness of the country.

Now the noise grated on her last nerve. She had no patience with people. She was miserable. They had welcomed her back to work and yet she didn't much care about her job any longer.

Working in a museum, she once hoped to run it with her

liberal arts degree, but now she didn't care. It was a job. She worked her hours and then she went home to an empty apartment that wasn't much bigger than the large bedroom that she'd shared with Trevor and Luis. The large bedroom where they had fucked for hours until they were all sated and worn out.

They had treated her with so much care and support. The time with them had been magical and she would always remember it as a beautiful period of her life. Until that last morning when Luis spoke how he truly felt.

That last day had been gut wrenching, and getting on that plane, she'd felt like a zombie walking to her assigned seat. Wishing she could sleep and hurting so much, she sat and stared into the dark sky, searching for an answer.

But it was better that she learned now that he didn't want children than after they were together and her heart was fully involved.

She'd spoken to Kalie and asked her to not give her phone number or address to them. She didn't want them showing up here and trying to convince her to come back.

A week had passed, and with each day, she kept telling herself soon she would feel better, but so far, just the thought of them brought tears to her eyes.

Walking down the street from the subway station, she stopped at the local pizza joint and picked up a sausage and cheese. The last week, she'd immersed herself in movies and books and everything she could to keep her mind occupied. Anything to pass the time between work and sleep.

And when the thought of Luis and Trevor crept in, she quickly pushed them out of her mind. Right now, it hurt too much to think about them.

Opening her apartment door, she threw the mail on the table and set her pizza down. Then she went into the bedroom and put on her pajamas.

Tonight she had ordered a book from her favorite author and after her dinner of pizza and wine, she would indulge in a romance where there was a guaranteed happily ever after. Where the men were not afraid of marrying and having children. Where the heroine would get the happiness she deserved.

With a sigh, she glanced through the mail and then opened the bottle of wine. The memory of the champagne bottle and how Luis had poured it over her body came to mind and she quickly shoved it out of her thoughts.

She'd save that memory for another time and another day when she could remember it without her heart shattering, her body aching for their touch, and her mind screaming to call them.

Just no.

It would never work. Time to move on. Let her heart heal.

Sitting at the table, she heard a knock at the door. Probably someone selling something useless.

Getting up, she walked to the door and opened it without checking the viewer.

Her heart plummeted to her feet at the sight of Luis and Trevor.

What were they doing here? She couldn't handle them trying to persuade her to change her mind.

"We want to talk," Trevor said.

"There's nothing left to say," she said.

"Yes, there is," Luis replied. "We flew all the way from Texas. Can't you at least give us five minutes?"

With a sigh, she opened the door farther, remembering she was in her pajamas. Oh well, they'd seen her in even less. But this felt more intimate.

"Have a seat," she said, pointing to her couch. The pizza box was on the table. "Would you like a slice of pizza?"

"Yes," Trevor said. "I'm starving because someone wouldn't stop to eat before we got over here."

She fixed them each a plate and then sat in a chair across from them.

For a few minutes, it was silent as they ate. When they were finished, she picked up the plates and put them in the sink.

"What do you want to discuss?"

Luis licked his lips. "The morning you got so upset, I spoke to my mother. She reminded me how I wanted children before I went into the Navy. She explained that most women want children. And then she told me to get home because you were probably on your way out the door. And you were."

Trevor sighed. "I didn't know you'd left. I was too busy speaking to my mother and talking her off the ledge regarding my younger brother who had decided he wanted to become a cage fighter."

Stacy couldn't help herself, she smiled. "A cage fighter? Really?"

"Yes, but don't worry, he's already had his face busted up and decided that's not for him. He's now talking about going into the service and I think that's a good place for him. I love my family. As crazy as they are, I want them to have a better life than me.

"And I want a wife and children. You reminded me that was the reason I've worked so hard to get where I'm at. To give my children a better life than I had growing up," he said. "I've spent the last week in Houston working at my company and visiting with my family. I needed to decide if Luis and I could remain partners."

She nodded. But they still had not said what she needed to hear before she agreed to continue seeing them. She wasn't going to go through this hurt again if they didn't want a true family. It was more than she could bear.

Luis stood and began to pace her small apartment. "The day you left, Trevor also left. I was alone and I crawled inside a bottle of scotch. While I was drunk, either my mind played a trick on me or my best friend returned from the dead. You see the reason I have episodes and return to that battle is because John took a bullet meant for me. We were in the jungles of Africa on a secret mission. We were fighting a group of Russian soldiers called The Wagner Group. They're vicious killers and we had them holed up in a little town where they were stealing diamonds from the locals."

Taking a deep breath, tears welled in his eyes. "One snuck up behind us. John stepped behind me and raised his gun. He took a bullet to the chest that was meant for me. He killed the soldier, but he died protecting me."

For a moment, he closed his eyes like pain was washing over him before he opened them and stared at her. "I've felt guilty ever since. He was my wingman, and because of him, I'm still alive. He came back and said to me, 'I'm dead, but you're alive. Don't fuck up the life you have. Make a decision and learn to live with it. Time to get over my death, Luis, and live your life. Don't disappoint me, soldier.'"

Stacy gasped. She couldn't imagine someone taking a bullet for her and then having to live with the thought that they weren't alive because of her. And then to be told not to fuck up the life they were leading was something she couldn't imagine.

"I've gone back to the Navy doctor who is working with me on my PTSD. I'm seeing him twice a week and he thinks he can help me. My mother believes that love can cure me as well," he said.

She was glad he was getting better. She hoped for his sake that the nightmares, the episodes, and everything ended and he had a peaceful life. But that wasn't what sent her running and he knew it.

"It's not the PTSD," she said. "We can deal with that. But I want a family. Those few days with you guys, I was falling in love with you and my heart can't just let you fuck me and not fall for you. And I need someone who is going to eventually want to marry me and have a family. It's been my dream since I was a little girl and I'm not giving it up. If you can't do that, then we're just wasting our time."

Tears welled in her eyes and she couldn't stop them from flowing down her cheeks. If they had come here to convince her to give up her dream, then they would only hurt her further. And she didn't need that right now.

Luis came over to her chair, pulled her up, sat, and then pulled her onto his lap. All the feelings rushed through her and she so wanted to lean into him, but she couldn't.

"Before I went into the Navy, I wanted children. Getting a vasectomy was so that no one would witness how I act when I have an episode. But the doctor seems to think he can cure me," he said.

For a moment, she felt hope. But then she couldn't take a chance. "But what if he can't. What if you still have episodes, then what? I'm not willing to give up my dream of a family. A large family with lots of little ones."

Why couldn't he understand that?

"Stacy, I love you. This past week has been miserable without you. I'll do whatever you want to make you happy. Trevor and I want to make a life with you. We want to see a baby in your belly. We want the sound of children running through the house."

She watched in stunned disbelief as Trevor suddenly dropped to one knee. "Stacy, we haven't known each other long, but we've lived a lifetime already. We're certain that you're the one for us. In a week, we fell in love with you. With your spunk, your determination, and your willingness to fight for what you want. We want you to marry us, have babies with us, and create the family you so desperately want. Please say you'll be our wife and marry us as soon as possible."

Trevor opened a ring box that held a stunning emerald-cut diamond surrounded by lots of little stones.

Unable to stop herself, she started crying, her chest aching and filling with the love she had for these men. Could this be true? Was it really happening for her?

"Yes, please, I want to marry both of you and have the family I have always dreamed of. I love you both so much and I've been miserable here without you."

Luis grabbed her cheeks and pulled her lips to his and kissed her deeply. "Thank God. I love you so much, Stacy, and this week has been terrible with you gone."

Trevor grabbed her hands and pulled her to her feet. He kissed her deeply, his mouth moving over hers like he was desperate to hang on to her.

"You're ours. You were made for us and we want you to return with us to Texas. We'll get married as soon as possible."

Laughing, she took each man's hand. "I never dreamed that taking a chance with you guys would be the best possible thing that ever happened to me. Luis, I have one condition. You must continue to see the doctor."

Trevor laughed. "I won the bet. I told him you were going to insist that he continue."

"I just want you to be healed and happy and to be the best possible man and father to our children."

Standing, he pulled her to him. "And I want that as well. Where in the hell is the bedroom in this place? I can't wait another minute to get inside you."

A giggle escaped her and she grabbed both of their hands and led them to her tiny bedroom with a queen mattress. Nothing like the super king-size bed they had, but it would do for tonight.

Stacy's heart overflowed with love for these two cowboys she'd found. "You two are the loves of my life. I can't wait any longer for the both of you to claim me."

They both pulled back and smiled.

Quickly she removed her pajamas.

"When we move you to Texas, I think you can donate your pajamas to Goodwill."

A smile filled her face and love overflowed from her heart. "I won't need pajamas as a married woman?"

"Not our wife," Trevor said as he removed his clothes.

She lay back on the bed and Trevor came to her side while Luis crawled between her legs.

"Are you certain you're ready? I found the last butt plug beside your note," he said.

"I wasn't going to wear it through security at the airport. It might cause some interesting questions," she replied.

"We don't want to hurt you. We want you to enjoy being between us," Luis said.

"Yes, Luis, I want the two of you to claim me. Make me yours. It's time. I need you both tonight at the same time."

Trevor caressed her face. "We love hearing you say that. You're ours and now you are wearing our ring."

"Yes," she said, feeling the tears swell behind her eyelids. Tonight she'd come home exhausted and so damn depressed, only for life to give her everything she wanted.

She leaned up and kissed his mouth, needing to feel connected to him in every way. Sure, she was a little nervous about taking them both at once, but she loved them. And she had no doubt they would make this a pleasurable experience for her.

Luis's fingers slid between her folds and then he leaned down and put his mouth on her pussy. Spirals of pleasure sizzled through her at the feel of his tongue as it caressed her intimately, delving inside her, finding her G-spot.

This man always knew how to make her come, and even now, she could feel the desire filling her.

Her fingers gripped the bed coverlet and she moaned deep in her throat as his teeth nibbled on her clit and an explosion of pleasure zipped through her body as her hips lifted off the bed to give him deeper access.

"Oh," she cried. "Luis, do that again."

"Anything you need, darling," he promised.

He chuckled and his teeth scraped across her clit as his hands slid beneath her hips, lifting her until she was firmly in his grasp, his mouth covering her pussy. With his mouth and tongue, he caressed her as she clenched her fists, moaning.

Trevor was at her head and he moved over the top of her and put his cock against her lips. "Suck me, Stacy. I love the feel of your mouth against my cock. Tonight, I want it all from you. I've missed you so much, darling."

Opening her mouth, she felt his hard dick slide in and she sucked him in deeper, running her tongue over the bulbous head.

Trevor groaned and ran his hands through her hair and pulled her mouth against his crotch. All of his cock was in her mouth and she did her best not to gag as he moved her at his pleasure over his dick.

This was the life she could expect from this day forward until death did they part. Because they were her men, her soon-to-be husbands, she would never let them go.

Luis continued sucking and licking and nipping her clit and she thrashed about on the bed, needing to come, but knowing he wasn't ready for her.

He removed his mouth and she gasped around Trevor's cock. Luis slapped her pussy and she all but screamed around the cock in her mouth as the need to come vibrated through her.

"After I spank your pussy again, you may come," Luis said and she couldn't wait. The tension rose within her.

"And when you do, I'm going to come in your mouth," Trevor said as he held her head, moving her mouth at his pace while she did her best to keep up with him.

She tried to prepare herself for what was coming, but Luis's fingers stroked her and suddenly he spanked her and stars filled her eyes, not from the pain, but from the explosion as she came.

Pleasure engulfed her as she moaned around Trevor's cock, her body trembling from the orgasm as Trevor filled her mouth with his seed. Her body stiffened as she rode the crest of her orgasm.

With a sigh, she fell back to earth and knew this would not be the last time she came tonight.

For a moment, they didn't move as Trevor's cock fell from between her lips and Luis shuffled until he was lying beside her on the bed.

"Trevor is going to take your ass. I'm going to claim that pussy of yours and, darling, I'm not using protection. You want a baby and I hope tonight we give you one," Luis said, pulling her on top of him. "A little girl with your eyes. Or a little boy who looks like me."

"Luis," she said, tears welling in her eyes. "I want that too. I want that so much."

He lined up his rock-hard cock with her pussy and she felt him slowly push it inside her.

Even though she had just come, her body came alive again. "Promise me, it won't hurt."

Leaning over her back, Trevor stroked her ass. "Baby, I'll be as gentle as I can be. If it gets to be too much, let me know. We have all night, and even the rest of our lives, and I want this night to be special for you."

"Are you ready? Again?"

Trevor chuckled. "Darling, it's been a week since I've been with you. I'm hard as a rock and so ready to fuck you."

Warmth filled Stacy as she tried to prepare herself for them being inside her at the same time. It was her desire, what she'd fantasized, and though she was eager, she was also a little nervous.

"We want you to enjoy us both claiming you," Luis said with a groan. "We want you to be happy. You're our woman, soon to be our wife."

That was all she needed to hear as she pushed her ass out to feel Trevor's fingers slowly entering her, stretching her, filling her. He was going to make her feel so good.

"Get ready, baby," he whispered as he filled her with lubricant that he swirled around her little rosebud.

She felt his cock at her entrance and tensed.

"No, baby," Luis cooed to her as his fingers found her clit and he tweaked the hard nub as he pulled out his cock and waited patiently for Trevor to fill her. "Relax. Think of how good we're going to make you feel."

Taking a deep breath, she willed herself to relax and that's when she felt a fullness, stretching her.

"Oh, Luis, she's so tight, she's gripping my cock."

A whimper came from Stacy as Trevor filled her and yet there was no pain, only a stretching. And now she understood why they insisted on her wearing a butt plug.

"I'm almost there, baby. You're doing great. Soon, it's going to feel so good," Trevor encouraged her as he continued to push inside her.

Luis's mouth covered hers and his lips consumed hers taking control, his tongue commanding entry as it danced with her own. Then he pushed his cock inside her pussy and she felt a fullness much like when she wore the butt plug.

The feelings were overwhelming as she realized that both men were now encased inside her body. Both of her men were taking her at the same time. Both of the men she loved with all her heart. They were all one.

And soon they would be one in not only spirit, but she would take one of their names. All that mattered was that they wanted the same things in life.

Their lips came apart as Luis began to move inside her. Then Trevor, and soon they had a rhythm going of one man entering and the other man pulling out. Sensations coursed through her that she never dreamed of experiencing.

"Oh," she cried as her body enlivened with her nerves crawling with heat and fire as the flames of their union ignited around her. Sandwiched between them, she'd never felt more loved, more cared for, or more desired than at this moment.

"Are you all right?" Luis asked between gritted teeth. "We're not hurting you."

"No, I love the feel of both of you inside me," she cried. "But I don't know how much longer I can last. I'm so filled with love. With my men."

"You're damn straight we're your men. You're our woman. Don't ever forget it," Luis said.

Luis grabbed her head and pulled her mouth down to his. He kissed her with so much passion, she felt like she would explode any moment.

And then Trevor slapped her on the ass and she couldn't hold back any longer. She broke the kiss. "Oh, baby, do that again. I'm going to come."

"Go ahead, Stacy, you deserve to come," Trevor said and he hit her on the ass again.

A ripple of pleasure began in her center and traveled up

through her and she felt like she was going to pass out as darkness and then light flashed before her eyes.

She felt Luis's seed coat the walls of her pussy as he thrust into her one last time and then Trevor, followed him, slamming into her ass as she clenched her muscles to bring him pleasure.

"Stacy," Trevor cried as he filled her.

As both of her men came, she cried out as her body trembled and shook from the massive orgasm that took her from the earth to the sky and back again.

For a moment, they all tried to slow their breathing as the world righted itself and she felt first Luis's cock and then Trevor's slip from her body.

Trevor collapsed on the bed beside them, and the two men took her into their arms. Amazed, Stacy lay there wondering if their life would always be so good.

"I love you," she said softly. "And I can't wait for us to have a family."

Luis kissed her softly. "I love you, Stacy. But I can't wait to take you back to Texas and our bed. This one is a little small."

She laughed. "It's not a huge bed, like yours. It's just a queen."

"You're our queen," Trevor said. "Don't ever forget it."

She glanced between her two men. How had she gotten so lucky? Not just one man, but two who she felt certain would always take care of her. Who would love her until the end of their time. And she couldn't wait for their life together to begin.

CHAPTER 15

Camila Garcia was undercover at the latest Nash family wedding that included her brother. She'd come from the marshal's office in San Antonio. This little town was known for having two men marry one woman. She'd read up on history at the local law library at SMU University where her brother, one of the grooms, had put her through college.

Only one man married the woman, but they shared everything. She couldn't imagine a man sharing another woman, but then, hell, she had trouble keeping one man satisfied. Keeping two would be impossible.

The last man she'd left standing outside of a nightclub in Dallas, holding his balls between his hands. Men pulled stupid tricks on women.

And don't ever try to play an officer of the law. It never worked out well for you.

The current sheriff of Blessing, Texas, was Jordan Nash, and Ely Austin was his deputy. The Nash family had a long history of being peace officers here in the little town. But she was investigating suspected corruption.

And she wasn't one to put up with anyone disrespecting the law or using it to their advantage. Not with her new credentials as Marshal Camila Garcia.

"Excuse me, ma'am, you're under arrest," a man's voice said.

Whirling around, she gazed at him. "What for?"

"For being too damn beautiful," he said with a smirk.

Did men really believe these kinds of lines worked on women? Maybe back in her mother's day, but she'd seen too much even in her short time as a law officer to accept this kind of bullshit line.

"What are you going to do about it?" she said, wondering how far he would take this.

Another man walked up. "Franco, what are you doing?"

Another one of the Nash brothers. Though she didn't think he was in law enforcement yet.

"I'm arresting this woman for being too beautiful," he said, getting out a pair of handcuffs.

Her eyes narrowed and she wondered if he would be brave enough to try to use them on her.

What he didn't know was that she was trained in the art of combat and she could put him on the ground in a matter of seconds and take his handcuffs and use them on him. That plan she liked.

The second man gazed at her. "She is a pretty one. How do you know the bride and grooms?"

Now that was a good question, and if they were smart, it would scare these two idiots off. "I'm Trevor's sister."

The man chuckled. "Oh, that could be trouble."

"You're damn right it could be," she said, walking up to the man, she laid her fingers on his chest. He was way too young to be a peace officer with his face full of not-quite-man fuzz. He was a handsome one. It was a shame he couldn't come up with a better line.

If he was going to try to arrest her, he better get started.

"Franco, maybe we should find another suspect," the other young kid said.

"No, I like this one," he said. "She'll do quite nicely."

Camila smiled like she was drawing her prey into her lair. These two had no idea what was about to go down.

"You're under arrest," Franco said, his voice cracking.

Frankly, she liked her men older. With experience.

She felt him slip the handcuffs around her wrist. "And what do you plan on doing with me?"

"We're going to take you home, spread you out on the bed, and lick every inch of your beautiful skin."

She wanted to laugh, but that would hurt their young manly feelings. They would spill their load before they could get off first base.

Glancing back at the guests dancing the night away, she made sure no one was paying them any mind.

With trained ease, she slipped off the cuffs, spun around, and took the man to the ground. She slapped them on him, and before the other man could run, she snared his leg and had him grounded next to his friend.

She sat on his back, his wrists in her hands.

"Now, gentlemen, tell me how many times you've played this little game of yours and how often it works."

They were both silent as they lay on their stomachs in the grass.

"Uh, we're sorry. A lot of women like it," the one man said.

"Well, as a peace officer, I don't," she said.

A tall, handsome man wearing a cowboy hat and dressed in jeans came around the corner and shook his head. "What have you two idiots done now?"

They glanced up at the man and groaned.

"They're pretending to be officers and they were going to arrest me," she said.

The man gazed at her, his dark eyes traveling along her body. A heat she'd not felt in a long time caressed her.

"Jordan Nash," he said, stepping toward her. "Sheriff of Blessing, Texas, and this one is my stupid younger brother. The one beside him is my deputy's stupid younger brother."

She shook the man's hand, the heat spiraling up her arm and down into her center.

This was her suspect. The man she was here to investigate.

"Do you want to file charges against these two?" he asked seriously.

Staring down at them, she grinned and wanted to put the fear of God into them. "Well, they were going to spread me wide and lick every inch of my beautiful skin."

The kids on the ground groaned.

"I think he's a little too young to be making those kinds of promises," the sheriff said. "Hell, the boy is in college, but his maturity level is in junior high."

She laughed.

Another man came around the corner and shook his head.

"Kyle, I swear I'm going to take you out behind the barn. What did he do now?"

Jordan turned and shook his head. "He and Franco were harassing her."

The man gazed at her and she returned his stare. He must be the deputy. The other man she was to investigate.

When a child went missing and the law officers were the last to have seen her, it throws suspicion on them and their office. It was time to find out what happened to five-year-old Rena Taylor.

And that was what Camila was here to find out. Child trafficking was her specialty.

"Deputy Ely Austin," the man said, holding out his hand.

"Marshal Camila Garcia," she said. "I'm Trevor's sister."

The two men's brows rose as they stared at her.

Why did she like these two lawmen? They were her prime suspects. Yet they were strong with muscled forearms and faces that were so damn good-looking.

"I'm here for the wedding, but I'd love to visit your office."

The two men glanced at one another and frowned. "When?"

"Now," she said.

She could tell from their expressions that they were interested in more than just letting her tour their offices.

"Let's go," Jordan said. "The wedding is over and the reception has reached that stage where I like to leave."

A smile spread across her face.

"I'll follow you," she said.

"No, why don't you ride with us? We'll come back later and get your car."

She wasn't afraid of them. After all, she could take down a big man with ease. And she had her trusty pistol in a garter beneath her dress.

They were lawmen and even if she was going to investigate them, she did appreciate their big beefy arms and the way they carried themselves.

Besides, if her brother could get married and share a woman with another man, she might even be agreeable to trying out these two handsome lawmen.

What was the draw with two men for a woman? Besides the obvious oral sex. It just seemed so perverse and yet she was curious.

"Let's go," she said, walking toward the cars. "Oh, wait, what about your brothers?"

Jordan laughed. "They're just fine where they are. Might be good for them to learn not to play that stupid trick."

"Especially on a beautiful woman like yourself. They made promises they couldn't keep," Ely replied. "But we will be more than happy to make certain you have everything you need."

She licked her lips. Was she getting into something more than she bargained for? There were two of them to her one self. But she still wasn't afraid. And it had been a long time since a man had gazed at her the way these two were looking at her.

And it had been even longer since she'd enjoyed the company of a man between her legs.

COME HOME
TO THE
Lawmen
RETURN TO
BLESSING, TEXAS
BOOK 3
LACEY DAVIS

PLEASE LEAVE A REVIEW

Did you enjoy the book? Reviews help authors. I would appreciate you leaving a review at the retailer of your choice.

Follow Lacey Davis on Facebook.

Sign up for my newsletter at https://laceydavisauthor.com/mailing-list **and receive a free book.**

TWO COWBOYS' CHRISTMAS BRIDE

*A*nna Best never dreamed her life could go so wrong. Two weeks before Christmas, her uncle sold her to the local whorehouse. One evening before the madam of the house could sell off her virginity, she'd been drugged and abducted.

Now she found herself in a rough tow sack that smelled like potatoes being hauled around in the back of a wagon. Whoever opened this bag better be prepared, because she would come out fighting.

Anna was no simpering woman and she was aching to give a good tongue lashing. The bouncing of the wagon had jolted her awake to her head pounding, her wrists tied, her mouth covered, and stuffed in a bag.

Not exactly how she'd planned her escape from the brothel.

The wagon wheels came to a stop and she listened as two voices whispered in the darkness.

"Is this the right place," a female voice said.

"I think so," a young man replied.

"Come on, lift her out of the wagon and let's leave her on the doorstep."

Anna wanted to scream, but all she could do was make muted noises. Still, she could kick.

"Good thing you stuffed her mouth, Ma."

Ma? A woman was involved in her kidnapping?

Fury roared through her as they dragged the gunnysack along the back of the wagon. She kicked and flailed her legs trying to create as much havoc for them as possible.

"Stop moving, girl, or I will drop you right here in the dirt," the woman said quietly.

Where did she know that voice from?

Tiring, she stopped thrashing as they carried her then set her down on the cold ground.

"Let's go," the woman whispered in the darkness.

"Won't she freeze to death?" a young male voice asked.

"Not this one. The devil is strong within her," the woman said.

What? Did the woman believe she wanted to be taken to a whorehouse? To have her uncle, a family member, sell her? All she had asked for in life was a loving family. And look where that had gotten her.

Sold to a brothel.

As they walked away, the sounds of their retreating footsteps crunching on the ground sent fear slamming into Anna. Trembling, she lay balled up in the darkness, unable to discern where they left her. What if wild wolves or coyotes found her?

What if she died right here inside this bag?

The cold started to creep into the potato sack. In Blessing,

Texas, the winters were mild, but still she started to shake. It was December, not exactly a hot summer day.

Doubled over inside the bag, she didn't have room to stretch her legs and they were going numb. She rolled and came up against a hard surface. A barn? House?

Rocking inside the bag, she hit the wall.

Bang!

Did anyone live here? Did she want to find out?

Bang.

Bang.

Tiring, her shoulder throbbing, she heard a noise.

A door opened.

"What the hell?"

"Hold that lantern a little higher, Mack," a voice said.

"What's the note say?" a deeper male voice asked.

"Merry Christmas."

Anna's temper exploded. She writhed and screamed as much as she could inside the bag.

The men cursed. "Someone's in there."

With relief, she felt them untying the bag and pulling it down then lifting her to her numb feet. Her eyes were blinded by the light of the lantern.

"Oh my God, it's a woman."

"A damn fine-looking woman," the other man said.

Slowly her eyes adjusted to the light as she stared at two extremely handsome men standing in the doorway without shirts on. Muscled arms and chests with wisps of dark hair glowed in the warm light.

Who were these men and why had she been delivered here?

"Santa brought us an early Christmas present. A woman."

To Continue Reading Go To Your Favorite Retailer!

Lacey Davis is the *alter ego* of a USA Today, bestselling author who decided to dive headfirst into the world of sexy romance. Why? Because who doesn't love writing about hunky bad boys and fierce, fabulous women who know how to make them beg for more? With these sizzling stories, I'm here to deliver the kind of romance that will leave you reaching for a fan (or an ice bath—your choice).

If you're into bad boys who like to take charge and strong women who aren't afraid to shake things up, then you've come to the right place. These steamy reads will not only get your pulse racing but also have you cheering for these bold women as they tame their wild men—and leave them wanting more. Ready for a little fun? Come on in, the temperature's *just* right.

www.LaceyDavisAuthor.com
The End